Missing Memories

a quilting cozy

Carol Dean Jones

Text copyright © 2018 by
Carol Dean Jones

Photography and artwork copyright ©
2018 by C&T Publishing, Inc.

Publisher: Amy Marson

Creative Director: Gailen Runge

Acquisitions Editor: Roxane Cerda

Managing Editor: Liz Aneloski

Project Writer: Teresa Stroin

Technical Editor / Illustrator:
Linda Johnson

Cover/Book Designer: April Mostek

Production Coordinator:
Tim Manibusan

Production Editor: Alice Mace Nakanishi

Photo Assistant: Mai Yong Vang

Cover photography by Lucy Glover and
Mai Yong Vang of C&T Publishing, Inc.

Cover quilt: *The Fidget Quilt*, 2015,
by the author

Published by C&T Publishing, Inc.,
P.O. Box 1456, Lafayette, CA 94549

Library of Congress Cataloging-in-
Publication Data

Names: Jones, Carol Dean, author.

Title: Missing memories : a quilting cozy
/ Carol Dean Jones.

Description: Lafayette, California
: C&T Publishing, [2018] | Series:
Quilting cozy series ; book 8

Identifiers: LCCN 2018003520 |
ISBN 9781617457388 (softcover)

Subjects: LCSH: Quilting--Fiction. |
Missing persons--Investigation--Fiction.
| Retirement communities--Fiction.
| Retirees--Fiction. | GSAFD:
Mystery fiction.

Classification: LCC PS3610.O6224 M57
2018 | DDC 813/.6--dc23

LC record available at
https://lccn.loc.gov/2018003520

Printed in the USA

10 9 8 7 6 5 4 3 2

A Quilting Cozy Series

by Carol Dean Jones

Tie Died (book 1)

Running Stitches (book 2)

Sea Bound (book 3)

Patchwork Connections (book 4)

Stitched Together (book 5)

Moon Over the Mountain (book 6)

The Rescue Quilt (book 7)

Missing Memories (book 8)

Tattered & Torn (book 9)

Left Holding the Bag (book 10)

Beneath Missouri Stars (book 11)

Frayed Edges (book 12)

Dedication
In memory of Glorine Dean

Acknowledgments

I want to express my sincere appreciation to five very special people: Phyllis Inscoe, Janice Packard, Sharon Rose, Robin Palmer, and Joyce Frazier, all of whom have spent hours reading these chapters, bringing plot inconsistencies and errors to my attention, and providing me their endless encouragement.

Thank you, dear friends, for all your hard work and for bringing fun and friendship to what could otherwise have been a tedious endeavor.

Chapter 1

"Something's wrong, Charles."

Sarah and Charles were returning from a two-week vacation in Colorado, where they'd been visiting Charles' two sons. "What is it?" her attentive septuagenarian husband asked, turning to help her position the travel pillow behind her head.

"No, not my pillow," she responded still groggy from her short nap. She waved his hand away. "It's something with the plane I think," she muttered. "I don't know ... I just have this feeling. ..."

"You drifted off, honey. You must have been dreaming. The plane is fine, and we're almost home," he responded reassuringly. Spotting the flight attendant moving in their direction, he waved his arm to get her attention. "Miss," he called to her. "Could you bring my wife a cup of herbal tea?" Although he didn't care for tea himself, especially herbal, he knew she often steeped a pot when she was anxious or worried. And even though she'd never admit it, traveling by air always caused her to become apprehensive.

"Certainly, sir," the attendant responded, looking over at the man's companion and noting a look of concern. "Are you okay, ma'am?"

"I guess I was dreaming," she responded reluctantly. "It's just … oh, it's nothing. A cup of tea would be nice. Thank you." She gave the flight attendant a warm smile and settled back into her seat.

"Did you have a good time?" Charles asked his wife once she appeared to be wide awake. This had been an important trip. He and Sarah were visiting his two sons whom he'd been estranged from since their teens. Over the past year, and with Sarah's help, he had begun rebuilding a relationship with both John and David, but this was the first time they saw one another on his sons' turf.

"I had a fantastic time, Charles. Your sons are such fine young men, and I love John's wife. Donna and I had great fun wandering through the shops while you and your boys were surfing the countryside in those snowmobiles."

"You should have come," he said shaking his head. "You missed a barrel of fun out there in the mountain wilderness."

Sarah was in excellent physical shape for a woman in her seventies, but she had vehemently refused his invitation to join them. "I had just as much fun as you did, and I was nice and warm in an elegant retail mall filled with boutiques the likes of which I've never seen."

"I know, but I wondered why you came home without the cowboy boots you said you were going to buy."

She gave him a sly look and said, "Don't be so sure I didn't buy them."

"Not the thousand dollars ones, I hope?"

"We'll see," she teased and turned to look out the window. "Look, we're approaching Middletown, and I think I can see Cunningham Village. Isn't that it right over there?" she said, pointed to a community far below them. Sarah and Charles had met not long after they each had moved into the retirement village, Charles recovering from a massive stroke and Sarah at her children's insistence a few years after her husband's death. Charles leaned across her to look and nodded.

"I'll be glad to get home," she mused, still looking down as Middletown grew larger below them. As nice as it was to be traveling and getting to know her husband's family, she missed the home they had built together and her friends in the village. Looking over at her husband with a smile, she added, "And I know Barney and Boots will be excited to have us home."

"I called Andy last night and told him we'd stop by for Barney on our way home," Charles responded. Their neighbor's daughter, Caitlyn, was taking care of their pets. She went to their house daily to feed and play with their cat Boots but kept Barney, their dog, at her house for the duration.

"How's Barney doing?"

"Andy said he's having a ball. Caitlyn's been taking him to the dog park twice a day and stopping for Emma along the way so he'd have a playmate." Both Barney and Emma were rescues. Sarah got Barney when she first moved to the village, and Emma was adopted by Sarah's best friend, Sophie. For the two dogs, it was love at first sight.

By the time they disembarked and walked to the luggage kiosk, Sarah's enthusiasm about returning home had escalated. She excitedly looked around for her son, Jason, who had agreed to pick them up but didn't see him. Moments later she was surprised to see her best friend's son, Timothy, and his fourteen-year-old daughter hurrying toward them.

"Sorry we're late," Timothy huffed, greeting Sarah with a kiss on the cheek and offering Charles a welcoming hand-shake. "We got waylaid watching the planes take off and land," he added.

"Penny," Sarah exclaimed, "I didn't expect to see you here. I'm so glad you came." Turning to Tim, she asked, "But why are you two here instead of Jason? Is everything okay?" Sarah had spoken with her son the night before their flight and had confirmed that he would be picking them up.

"He called me this morning," Timothy explained, "and asked if I was available to pick you folks up. He said he'd like to go with Jennifer to her doctor's appointment this afternoon."

"Is she sick?" Sarah asked with concern. "Jason didn't say a word about it yesterday when we spoke."

"It's nothing to worry about. Jason said it was just a routine appointment." Sarah saw him pinch in a smile as he turned away.

"Are you boys keeping something from me?"

Timothy chuckled, finding it amusing that Sarah and his own mother still called him a boy despite the fact he was well into his fifties. "I've told you everything I'm allowed to say," he responded. Sarah couldn't miss the twinkle in his eye as he hurried to catch up with Charles. *He's holding something back*, Sarah thought. *And I'll just bet I know what it is.*

As Timothy and Charles were walking toward the parking lot with the luggage, Sarah hung back in order to call her son. There was no answer at home, so she dialed his cell phone. She caught him at the grocery store where he explained they had stopped on their way home. Jason sounded particularly cheerful. "Jennifer's on the other side of the store looking for something in a box that we can stick in the oven for dinner," he explained. "I didn't want her to be fussing over a meal tonight."

"So tell me about Jenny's doctor appointment. Is something wrong?"

"Oh no, Mom, absolutely not," he insisted with a light-heartedness uncommon to her rather serious-minded son. "She's just fine. Would you like to speak to Alaina?" and without waiting for her response, he put the phone to his daughter's ear and said, "Talk to Grandma."

Her two-year-old granddaughter said a few words but sounded reluctant. Sarah could picture her rubbing her eyes with her fist and looking down like she did whenever she was asked to perform in some way. "Well, Alaina, I'll see you tomorrow when you and your parents come to my house for lunch, okay?"

"Okay," Alaina said barely above a whisper.

"And Barney will be there too," Sarah added. The child giggled and said something to her father. Alaina and Sarah's dog, Barney, had been fast friends from the day they met.

"Kitty too?" Alaina asked, returning her attention to the phone.

"Yes, Boots will be there too," Sarah assured her granddaughter, but she couldn't promise Alaina that she would see the cat. Boots had taken up residence on top of the kitchen cabinets and only came down for meals and to wander the house once everyone was asleep. Boots had escaped to the top of the kitchen cabinets the previous year when the washer flooded, and she obviously liked it there. Concerned for the cat's comfort, Charles had moved her bed and blankets up there for her, but Sarah still required that Boots come down for meals.

Jason took the phone back, and they discussed arrangements for the next day. "Okay, we'll see you then," he said abruptly and ended the call.

Sarah disconnected and stared at the phone for a moment. As a smile spread across her face, she said aloud to herself, "Do you suppose …?" but she vowed to keep her suspicions to herself.

Having reached the parking lot, Timothy and Charles were so deeply engrossed in conversation about the Colorado Rockies game that Charles and his sons had attended at Coors Field the previous weekend that the two men walked right past the car. "Hey, you two," Sarah called out, winking at Penny who had stayed behind with her. "Let's take the car. It's too far to walk."

They both turned, looking momentarily confused but immediately realized what they had done and wheeled the suitcases back to the car.

"Thanks for picking us up, Tim," Sarah said once they were seated in the car. She was sitting in the front with Timothy so that Charles and Penny could continue their conversation about the planes she had seen with her father. Charles, having flown in the service, could answer many of her questions.

"So," Timothy began once he had merged onto the highway leading to their home in Middletown, "How was your trip?"

"It was delightful," Sarah responded. "I love the Denver area, and his boys treated us to all the tourist attractions."

"You have boys?" Penny asked, suddenly attentive to what Sarah was saying and waiting with anticipation for Charles' response.

Timothy quietly moaned in the front seat and mouthed the words, "Oh no. Boys!" Sarah laughed and whispered. "Don't worry. We're all here for you, Timothy. We'll get you through it."

"Well, yes, I have boys," Charles was saying, "but they're grown men in their forties."

"Oh," Penny responded, sounding disappointed. "That's really old."

Charles laughed and said, "Yeah, I guess forty is pretty ancient. I probably shouldn't point out that I'll be twice that old in a couple of years."

Penny looked at Charles in awe. "Really?"

Timothy and Sarah rode in silence for the next few miles, each lost in their own thoughts while occasionally tuning into the chatter in the back seat. After a while, Sarah said, "I'm glad you brought Penny. She's a delightful young girl. How's she doing in school?"

"She's doing just great," Timothy responded. "I know she misses her mother, but she's made friends, and she loves being with all of us. She's coming right along," he said with a proud smile. "I'm still hoping I can do this...."

"You've become an excellent father, Tim," Sarah responded, squeezing his arm and glancing back at the young girl who was excitedly telling Charles about the progress her new puppy was making.

Timothy had been a bachelor all his life. The previous winter he had retired from the Alaska pipeline and was making plans to return to his home in Middletown when he received a call from his old girlfriend, saying that she needed to talk to him. He and Betsy had gone their separate ways many years before when she insisted on living off the grid in Alaska, and he knew he wanted to return home to a more comfortable life. What she hadn't told him at the time was that she was pregnant with his child.

When he arrived at her isolated cabin, he had been greeted by a shy teenager named Penelope, whom he later learned should only be addressed as Penny.

As it turned out, Betsy had wanted to see him because she was dying of cancer and was eager to make a plan for her daughter. Their daughter.

Timothy didn't have to think twice about it. He had immediately arranged to get Betsy moved into a hospice facility and moved Penny into the spare room in his Anchorage apartment. Betsy died a few weeks later, and soon after the funeral, the two had flown to Middletown— Timothy's home, and what was soon to become Penny's home as well.

They had been greeted warmly by his mother and her network of friends, all of whom assumed responsibility for guiding Timothy into his new role as a father. Timothy and Penny lived with Sophie for a few months but soon moved into their own home and established themselves as a family of three: Timothy, Penny, and an adorable puppy named Blossom.

"Colorado is a beautiful state," Charles said, abruptly bringing Sarah out of her reverie. "I think we should plan to vacation there more often, don't you, dear?"

"I agree," she responded turning in her seat so she could see him. "And I loved getting to know your family." She and Charles had only been married a couple of years and were still finding their places in each other's family.

"You'd already met Charles' sons, hadn't you?" Timothy interjected.

"Yes, they've both been here, but I hadn't met John's wife or his son, Jimmy."

"Is his other son married?"

"David? No, but we met the lovely woman he's been seeing and it wouldn't surprise me if we're back in Colorado within the year attending their wedding. They seem to be very much in love."

"John's the attorney, right?" Timothy asked.

"Yes, you met him when he was here helping Charles with that legal matter a couple of years ago."

"Legal matter?" Charles exclaimed. "Legal matter?" he repeated a little louder, pretending to be offended. "Aren't you trivializing the significance of my plight? Don't you mean that he was here saving me from a lifetime of incarceration?"

Sarah laughed. "Now I think you're exaggerating the significance of what you call your plight."

"Well, whichever it is, we couldn't have gotten along without him," Charles responded.

"True. And it was a turning point in your relationship with both of your sons."

"Absolutely," Charles replied with a satisfied smile. "Absolutely."

Chapter 2

"So, tell me all about your trip," Sophie, Sarah's best friend and neighbor, was saying as she joined Sarah at the kitchen table where she had placed a freshly baked coffee cake and a steaming pot of coffee. "And did you go to any fabric stores?" she added eagerly.

Sarah burst out laughing. "Sophie, I can hardly believe that's you." Sophie had shown no interest in learning to quilt despite Sarah's encouragement. At least not until the past winter when she discovered that quilts could be made by hand. She had shown no interest at all in buying a sewing machine nor in learning to use one at the quilt shop, but while reluctantly attending one of Sarah's quilt club meetings, Sophie had met a woman who offered to teach her how to piece by hand.

Sophie, being a knitter herself and very competent with handwork, had taken to it immediately and had begun piecing a table runner for herself. She later signed up for several appliqué classes at the quilt shop and was able to complete a very intricate wall hanging, which featured a vase of flowers in the center surrounded by intertwined vines of ivy.

"Well, to answer your question," Sarah began, "I did get to two fabric stores in Denver and another one on our day trip to Colorado Springs. In fact," she added reaching into her tote bag, "I brought you something."

Sarah pulled the kit out of her bag and handed it to her friend. Sophie's eyes sparkled with excitement as she exclaimed, "Oh my! That's beautiful." But moments later Sarah saw her excitement begin to fade as she looked at the gift more closely. The kit contained all the materials and instructions for making a lap quilt. The blocks were eight-inch squares of neutral fabrics. There was a very pale green sashing between the blocks and an eight-pointed star in each intersection as cornerstones. The stars were pictured in soft pastel colors. What made the quilt spectacular were the beautiful, vividly colored flowers appliquéd in each block: rosebuds, tulips, carnations, and peonies, each with a stem and leaves, one with a small blue bird resting on the stem.

"But Sarah," Sophie objected. "This is way out of my league. There's no way I could make this quilt."

"Here's my plan," Sarah began. "We'll cut out the eight-inch squares—all the fabric is in this kit. Then you'll begin appliquéing the flowers onto the fabric squares while I cut the sashing and make the star cornerstones. When you've finished your appliqué, you and I will put the quilt together, and I'll do all the machine sewing. You can pin and press. What do you think?"

Sophie looked like she was about to weep with excitement. "Oh, Sarah, I love the idea, and I love it that this quilt will be made by the two of us. Who would have ever thought it?" she marveled, looking again at the picture on the front of the kit. "You really think I can do this?"

"I know you can. You're very skilled with the needle and your appliqués are beyond perfect."

"And you don't mind doing the machine work for me?" she asks almost timidly.

"I want to do it. This will be fun, and I've hoped that you and I could make quilts together, but I didn't really think it would ever happen. Grab your calendar and we'll schedule our first sewing bee."

"I don't need my calendar. How about right now?"

Sarah laughed and started to suggest another time but, realizing how excited Sophie was, she agreed to start it today. "Let's head over to my house," she responded, "so we can use my cutting board and rotary cutter. We'll get the backgrounds cut, and you can start your appliqué anytime you want. In fact, why don't you bring it to the club meeting tonight? I know the girls would love to see it, and you can work on it there."

"Good idea. Delores can give me pointers. I might need a refresher course for those thin stems."

They took Sophie's car back to Sarah's house. Although she'd had her knee replacement, it was still difficult to walk uphill, and there was a gentle incline all the way from her house to Sarah's. "Hey," Sophie said suddenly. "You never got around to telling me about your trip."

"Stay for dinner tonight and Charles and I can tell you about it together. We'll be eating early since the quilt club meeting starts at 7:00."

* * * * *

"Welcome home, Sarah," several members of the Friday night quilting group called out in unison as Sarah walked into Running Stitches, her local quilt shop. Most of the regular members were already there when Sarah and Sophie arrived: Christina and Kimberly, sisters and long-arm quilters; Allison, the newest member of the group; Delores, a very experienced quilter and occasional teacher in the shop; Caitlyn, Andy's sixteen-year-old daughter and youngest member of the group; Ruth, the owner of the shop; and Ruth's sister Anna who had moved to Middletown to be near her sister and to work part-time in the shop. Anna's husband, Geoff, was also in the shop working on the computer.

"Thank you, everyone. It's good to be home," Sarah responded, spotting Anna's little girl, Annabelle, on her mother's lap. "Do I see a new member?" Sarah asked, heading toward the little girl. "Hi, Annabelle."

"She came in with her daddy, and she's going home just as soon as he's finished." Just as Anna spoke, Annabelle wiggled to get out of her mother's arms, but Anna was able to hang onto her. "Geoff, are you about finished? We're starting the meeting. …" Turning to the group, she added, "I need a break from this child. You wouldn't believe the amount of energy and curiosity she has." Everyone nodded and Delores lifted the child onto her lap. Annabelle immediately became very still and covered her face with her chubby little hands as if she were suddenly shy.

"It's a difficult time, but hang in there, Anna," Delores said attempting to reassure the young mother.

"Yes," Ruth teased. "You still have the teens to get through."

Turning her attention toward Sarah and Sophie, who were now seated at the large worktable, Ruth said, "So, Sarah, tell us about your trip," but before Sarah could speak, Christina spoke up asking, "And did you buy any fabric?"

Sarah chuckled and said, "Funny, that's just what Sophie asked me. I guess that really is the most important part of any vacation." Sarah told them about the two shops she visited in Denver, and Sophie pulled out her kit from the Colorado Springs shop and explained their plan for completing it.

Delores, who had been Sophie's teacher, looked at the pattern more closely than the rest of the group and assured her she'd be able to do the appliqué. "If you need any help, just holler," she added.

"Caitlyn, I see you have a shopping bag from Colorado. What do you have there?"

"Sarah brought this for me," Caitlyn responded as she reached into the bag and pulled out a pattern. "It's a Triple Irish Chain," she said timidly. Caitlyn was the youngest member of the group but was proving to be a very creative quilter.

"I brought it because I wanted to ask you what you think of this idea." She reached into the bag again and pulled out two bags of assorted scraps. "She also brought me these two scrap bags of floral fabric, and instead of making three solid chains like in the picture, I'd like to make all the chains with a variety of florals. Do you think that would look okay?" she asked tentatively.

"It would be like a wide row of color wash crisscrossing the quilt instead of distinct chains," Ruth responded thoughtfully, "but, you know, I think I like it."

"I do too," Delores added. "Let's take a look at the fabrics."

Caitlyn began pulling the small cuts of fabrics out of the bags. "They're all flowers," she said. The group picked through the fabrics and began to sort them into piles of small, medium, and large prints.

"Will you use just certain colors?"

"I'd like to use them all if you think it would look okay...."

"Just like a summer garden," Anna called over her shoulder as she handed Annabelle off to Geoff and gave her a quick kiss on the cheek.

"You'll need more fabric," Delores added. "I have lots of florals, and I suspect everyone else does too." Turning to the group, she suggested that they all bring some scraps in for Caitlyn.

"What size do you want?" Kimberly asked. "Christina and I have loads of scraps."

"The pattern calls for two-and-a-half-inch strips."

"Check in the back room, too," Ruth suggested. "There are lots of floral fabrics in our scrap barrel. You're welcome to help yourself."

"Would you like for us to help you with the quilt?" Christina asked. "We could cut and sew strips for you at our next meeting." Everyone waited for Caitlyn's response, not wanting to intrude if it was something she wanted to do by herself.

"Oh, that would be great. That way I can get started right away. You know, with school and all, I don't have lots of time for sewing."

"Is this quilt for you or is it a gift?"

"I have someone in mind I'd like to give it to, but I'm not saying yet," she responded tentatively.

Delores smiled and glanced at Sarah. *It's nice having a young person in the group.*

Christina and Kimberly pulled out the charity quilt the group had made for the women's shelter. The sisters had completed the quilting on their long-arm machine, and Delores offered to put the binding on. Several others shared what they were working on, and the group spent the rest of the meeting huddled in the storage room searching through the two barrels of fabric and pulling out floral fabrics.

As they were packing up to leave, Ruth said, "Wait a minute! We never heard about Sarah's trip to Colorado!"

"Too late now," Sarah laughed as she picked up her tote bag. "Anyway, we talked about the most important part—the fabric. I'll tell you all about the rest of the trip while we cut fabric next week."

As the group was leaving, Ruth motioned Sarah aside. "Can you stay for a few minutes, Sarah?" Ruth asked. "I have a proposition for you."

"Sounds interesting," Sarah replied. She looked outside and saw that Sophie was getting into the van. Sarah waved to her indicating that she'd be right along.

Ruth pulled out a brochure describing a national quilt show coming to Chicago and asked Sarah if she'd like to accompany her as a guest of the shop. "You've done so much for me by teaching classes, and I'd like to offer this little bonus. Of course, there's one catch," she added with a sly grin. "I'd like for you to manage the booth for a few hours each day while my friend and I take in the show and have lunch, but otherwise you'll be on your own to enjoy the show."

Sarah asked a few questions about the logistics and said she'd love to do it.

"So you'll come!" Ruth exclaimed.

"Absolutely, Ruth, and thank you. The last time I went to a quilt show with you I ended up having to come home on the first day and never had a chance to see the quilts."

"I remember. Problems with your daughter, Martha, as I recall. How is she doing, by the way?"

"She's just fine, and we're happy about the connection she's made with Sophie's son. Timothy's a fine man, and I know he'll be good to her. Her first marriage, as you may remember, was a disaster, and she's been overcautious ever since."

"As was her mother, as I recall," Ruth joshed.

"Yes, as was her mother," Sarah agreed, looking slightly embarrassed. "I admit it, but I got over it, didn't I?"

"You sure did. Now, as for the show, I promise not to work you to death. The show is for three days, and I'll only need your help for a short block of time each day, so you'll have plenty of time to enjoy the quilts and take as many classes as you want. The Chicago show always attracts excellent instructors."

"Don't you think you'll need full-time help in your booth?

"Yes, and I have that covered. My friend Tessa is going to work with me every day. You've never met her, have you?"

"No, but I remember when you two went to the Kentucky quilt show together. You've known her for a long time, haven't you?"

"Yes, we've been friends since I first opened my shop. She had just opened her own quilt shop in Barlow, and when she read about my opening, she contacted me to offer some suggestions on how we could work together. Over the years, we've become close friends, although I don't see her very often." Ruth went on to explain that Tessa's shop was only an hour or so east of Hamilton. "We've run a few sales at the same time and offered incentives for quilters to visit both shops."

"Have you been to her shop?"

"Yes, I drove over to Barlow a couple of years ago and spent the weekend with Tessa. Her shop, Fussy Cuts, is small, probably only a few thousand bolts, but it's just delightful. She has a classroom in the back, and one of her retired friends teaches classes for her. She has sample quilts hanging on the walls to encourage new quilters to sign up for classes.

"I've never been to her shop," Sarah remarked, "but that's a cute name."

"Geoff has even offered to help her set up an online business or at least a website, but she seems reluctant to do it. She told me once she doesn't want to draw attention to herself, but I've tried to tell her that's part of having a business."

"She doesn't want to have her own booth at the show?"

"No, she's never had a booth, but she goes to the shows. We figured this would be a good way to spend some time together. She's preparing kits to sell at my booth, but she isn't bringing fabric. She'll be with me all three days, and I just might be able to slip away and take one of the classes. I've never been able to do that." Ruth handed the show schedule to Sarah, and they went over the classes briefly.

"Well, if you two want to take a class together, I'd be happy to take care of the booth," Sarah offered. "I'll have lots of free time. Will Anna manage your shop while you're away?"

"Yes, and Delores can help on the weekend. She's busy at the museum during the week, but I'm sure Anna can handle weekdays alone. If not, Nathan will come in." Ruth's husband often helped out in the shop, and the shoppers loved him. He was a handsome, soft-spoken man who had been raised in the Amish tradition, as was Anna before they married and left the community.

"Now exactly when is the show?" Sarah asked as she turned the brochure over, searching for the dates. "Oh, here it is. It's just a few weeks away, Friday through Sunday.

"We'd be driving up the night before. Look through that brochure and let me know what classes you want to take and I'll cover those costs too."

"Oh Ruth, you don't have to do that."

"It's a business expense," Ruth responded, dismissing Sarah's concern.

"Oh, my!" Sarah abruptly exclaimed. "I completely forgot that Sophie's waiting in the van. I've got to run."

The two friends exchanged a quick hug, and Sarah hurried to Sophie's van where she found her friend diligently appliquéing a small rosebud on an eight-inch square.

Chapter 3

S arah pretended to be surprised when Jason and Jennifer handed her the sonogram with a wide grin and sparkling eyes. "It's the first picture of your new grandchild," Jason exclaimed proudly.

Jennifer reached into her bag and pulled out a small album with the words *Grandma's Brag Book* printed on the cover. "And this is for you so you can get an early start."

Sarah gave her a warm hug and told her she already had another picture to put in the album. She reached for her phone and displayed a picture of Jennifer looking like a proud peacock. "Now that's a picture of a jubilant pregnant lady," Sarah announced.

"You knew, didn't you?"

"I couldn't miss it. You two have been just glowing for the past month. Now, sit down and tell me all about it."

She didn't say it to the happy couple, but Sarah couldn't help but hope it would be a boy. Jason lost his first son, Arthur, when he was only eleven. The stress had led to the breakup of Jason's marriage, and Sarah had been so happy when he announced his engagement to Jennifer several years later. Their only child, Alaina, was now two years old.

"Have you told Alaina yet?"

"No, you know how time drags for the young," Jason responded. "She'd never have the patience to wait six months."

* * * * *

The next three weeks seemed to fly by for Sarah, and it was suddenly time to leave for Chicago. Charles was loading her suitcase and supplies into the car while Sarah put a few finishing touches on the food she'd prepared for Charles. "Don't forget I was a bachelor for many years, my dear," he teased as he came into the kitchen from the garage. "I know how to make a few things for myself."

"Don't you fib to me, Charles Parker. I know you ate most of your meals in the Community Center cafeteria before you met me."

"Don't sell me short! I can boil hot dogs, make sandwiches, and I can even prepare a delicious beef stew."

"I know," she chuckled. "I watched you open the can the night you invited me to your apartment for a candlelight dinner."

Later that afternoon, as Charles and Sarah pulled up in front of Running Stitches, they saw Ruth heading out of the shop with an armload of fabric and Nathan on the ground behind their van hitching up their small cargo trailer.

Sarah leaned across the seat to kiss her husband goodbye, but Charles said, "I think I'll stay around and give them a hand."

Sarah smiled her appreciation and hopped out to join Ruth, who had placed the bolts of fabric in the trailer and was returning to the shop. "I've made quite a mess in here,"

Ruth was saying as she picked up another armload of bolts. "I'd better call Anna before we leave and ask her to come in early tomorrow so she can get the shop tidied up before she opens."

"I can begin straightening up now," Sarah offered.

"I'd rather you help me get the rest of the fabric out so we can get on the road. I'd like to get there before dark and before the other trucks and vans take all the best parking spots."

The two men got the trailer hitched up, and Charles, with the help of the instruction manual, checked to make sure the safety features were in place while Nathan carried the last of the fabric from the shop and arranged them in the trailer. "Is that everything?" he asked his wife.

"No, we need to load those boxes over there," She replied pointing to a stack of boxes filled with fabric. Turning to Sarah, she explained, "I cut one-yard and half-yard pieces of all my most popular fabrics. That way we won't need to spend all our time at the show cutting."

"How about the fat quarters we cut yesterday?"

"I've already put those boxes into the van, but would you please grab a few baskets. Fat quarters look pretty displayed in baskets, and we can store the extras under the table."

"Under the table?" Charles inquired suspiciously as he walked back into the shop. Sarah's husband was a retired detective with the Middletown Police Department and often acted like he was still on the job. "Are you paying your help under the table?"

"No, Charles," Ruth responded defensively. "I'm talking about the actual space *under the table*." After a pause, she added, "The show organizers supply tables and a white tablecloth that reaches all the way to the floor. I like to add a quilt over that for display, but their long tablecloths create lots of hiding space under the table for supplies. I'll keep a backup of fabric under there too."

"Sounds reasonable. Sorry if I was using my interrogation voice. Sarah is trying to break me of that." Looking around the room, his eyes settled on the pile of boxes, and he said, "I'll help Nathan with the rest of these boxes."

"Wait," Ruth called to him as he headed toward the trailer. "Would you see if there's room in the back of the van for those?"

"What about this box of patterns?" Sarah asked, also on her way toward the trailer.

"Those can go in the trailer, but," she added turning to her husband, "Nathan, would you pull that pile of quilts out of the trailer and put them in the van please?"

"With all the things you're taking in the van, I'm beginning to wonder why we own this trailer," Nathan groused, even though the small trailer was practically full with bolts of fabric, folding chairs, a wire display rack, two five-foot long wooden shelving units, and several boxes of sewing accessories.

"Just relax, dear husband," Ruth responded cheerfully. "I've done this before, you know. If I have those things in the car, I can begin setting up the booth while I'm waiting for someone to unpack the trailer."

"I know, I know," he responded good-naturedly. Ruth explained to Sarah later that, although Nathan grumbled about the show, he would be the first to admit that the exposure she gets for the shop at the shows was phenomenal, especially for their online business.

"How will we get all this unpacked?" Sarah asked, knowing that it had taken the four of them to pack it all up."

"That's the easy part," Ruth replied with a wide grin. "The convention center will already have our tables and dividers in place, and I've hired two strong young men to unpack the trailer. All we'll have to do is arrange the booth as they bring in the supplies. It's a piece of cake," she added with a chuckle.

Sarah heard Nathan continuing to complain but noticed that he held her close as they were saying goodbye. *Perhaps he grumbles because he'll miss her,* she thought with a smile as she looked around for her own husband.

"Are you sure you don't want me to come up for the day on Saturday? We could catch a show and go to dinner," Charles said as they were saying goodbye.

"That sounds like fun, but I'm going to be pretty busy," Sarah replied. "I've got classes all three days, and I've promised to handle the booth a few hours every day as well. Let's plan a weekend in Chicago for just the two of us sometime soon."

"Sounds good, but I'll miss you."

"I'll miss you too, but Barney needs you, so you go home and hold down the fort. We'll be back late Sunday night or Monday morning, depending on how tired we are once the show closes."

Sarah got settled in the passenger seat, and they pulled away from the curb, waving goodbye to their husbands. Charles was wearing his forlorn look, but Sarah knew he was smiling inside. She loved quilt shows, and he was in favor of whatever made her happy.

"So," Ruth said once they were on the interstate, "Tell me about your trip to Colorado. Denver, right?"

"Yes, we were in Denver most of the time. Both of his sons live within a few blocks of each other, but their lives are completely different. I think you met John when he was here. He's a criminal lawyer and has a nine-year-old son, Jimmy. John's wife, Donna, is quite a bit younger than John. He introduces her as his 'trophy wife' but not in a derogatory way. He says it with such love. They seem very happy."

"David isn't married, is he?"

"No, but he's been seeing a delightful woman. Stephanie's a good friend of Donna's, and the three of us had a shopping trip to die for while the men were touring the countryside on snowmobiles. Stephanie took us to this historic downtown area where they have trendy shops and chic runway fashions. It was cold, but we didn't care. We window shopped, poked around in boutiques, and even tried on a few outrageously expensive outfits."

"Did you bring any of those outfits home?" Ruth asked.

"I only bought one thing, a scarf. Well, it's more than a scarf. It's more like a fashionable shawl. It's cashmere, and I wore it with my black dress to a very elegant cocktail party at John's firm the night before we left."

"So, you had a good time?"

"I did. There was lots of sightseeing that I won't bore you with now, but I will later at the hotel. I brought pictures."

* * * * *

"They gave us a prime location," Ruth said excitedly when she found her assigned spot.

The convention center had provided three six-foot tables and Ruth had arranged for two more, all with white covers that hung to the floor. They pushed two of the tables together end to end along the back divider, creating a table space twelve feet long. Then they placed one table perpendicular on each end, forming a wide U-shaped booth. Sarah pulled the remaining table a few feet in front of their booth to be used as a cutting table.

Once the two women had the tables placed, Ruth cocked her head to the side and surveyed the new arrangement. "This looks good," she finally announced. "We'll use the two in the middle for bolts and the ones extending on the sides for pre-cut pieces, and Tessa's kits."

"What about the wooden shelves that Nathan built?"

"We'll set those side by side on the back of the center tables, and that will give us a twelve-foot long shelf for displaying fabric."

"I like that," Sarah responded, "except we need more space here to allow for the traffic pattern. You and I are already bumping into one another," she added laughing. They pulled the cutting table farther away from their merchandise tables and finally agreed that they were pleased.

The boys Ruth had hired to unpack the trailer weren't due for another hour, but the two women had brought enough items in from the van to begin setting up the booth. They placed quilts across several of the tables and hung the rest on the dividers which had the effect of completely encompassing their space in quilts.

Sarah placed baskets in an appealing arrangement on the side tables and began unpacking the fat quarters and arranging them in and around the baskets.

"When the boys bring the rotating display rack in, let's put it over here and fill it with patterns and books."

"Good idea," Ruth responded from under one of the tables where she was storing the boxes of extra pre-cut fabrics. By the time the young men arrived to unload the trailer, they had the booth ready. Ruth asked them to bring the two wooden shelves in first so they could place all the bolts right where they wanted them as they came in.

By 8:00 that night, Ruth and Sarah stood back and looked at the booth with pleasure. "Perfect!" Ruth announced. "I think we have a very appealing booth."

"What time are you expecting Tessa?" Sarah asked.

"She said she'll try to get here an hour or so before the show opens at 10:00. You never know about traffic coming in this direction, though. As long as she's here for the opening bell, I'll be happy."

"I'll stick around until she arrives," Sarah offered. "My first class isn't scheduled until midafternoon. I plan to spend the morning strolling around looking at quilts, and I might stop in the lecture hall for Marian Braydon's presentation.

"Good plan," Ruth responded. "If we're not too busy, I might leave Tessa in charge and sit in on that one myself. I love her work."

"Let's get some dinner and go to bed early," Sarah suggested, wanting to get to her room and call Charles before he went to bed. Both women were exhausted by the end of their very busy day but agreed that they were probably too wound up to sleep.

"I brought my electronic reader just in case."

Chapter 4

"I thought Tessa would be here by now," Ruth was saying apologetically. It was Friday morning, and the show had been open for an hour. Sarah was standing by in case she was needed, although they'd only had two visitors so far and neither one made a purchase. "You go on and have a good time. I can manage until she gets here."

Sarah looked at her watch and said, "I'll stay until she arrives. I have three days to enjoy the show, and you're going to need help. In fact, it looks like there's a customer headed this way right now."

Ruth looked up and gave out an excited squeal. "Henrietta!" Ruth hurried over and wrapped her arms around the elderly woman who was slowly heading their way with the help of an expensive-looking carved cane. "I had no idea you'd be here," Sarah heard Ruth saying. "Do you have a booth?"

"No, but my daughter does," the woman responded, "and I just came along to help out. I was so excited when I saw your name on the program," the woman continued, "and I had to find you. How long has it been anyway?"

"Over ten years, at least," Ruth replied, offering her arm and walking the woman over to her booth where Sarah had set up a folding chair. "Sarah, I want you to meet a very dear friend of mine. This is Henrietta Kirshner. Do you remember when I told you the story of how I happened to purchase the quilt shop? This is the wonderful lady who owned it before me. She taught me everything I know about running a shop," Ruth added, smiling down at her friend who was now sitting. "And Henrietta, this is my friend, Sarah Parker. She's teaching in the shop like I used to do in your shop."

Noticing that Henrietta appeared to be somewhat winded, Sarah offered her a bottle of water, which she gratefully accepted. "So Ruth worked for you in your shop?" Sarah responded.

"Yes, she was the best employee I ever had, but after my husband died, I decided to move up north to be close to my children."

"That's when I purchased the shop," Ruth interjected.

"I managed to go six months without a shop," Henrietta continued with a chuckle, "and that was all I could endure. I love being surrounded by fabric and having quilters coming and going all day. I opened a small shop up there and had it for another fifteen years. My youngest daughter, Adele, recently took it over."

"Do you miss it?" Ruth asked. She had pulled up the other chair and was sitting across from her old friend.

"I help out now and then. Oh, and I teach a couple of classes for Adele like you used to do, Ruth. We had fun, didn't we?" Before Ruth could respond, Henrietta stood up and said, "I've got to get over there and check out your fabrics. I see so many pretty things that I want to touch. . . ."

While the two friends visited, Sarah handled a couple of sales and noticed that another group of women was heading for their booth. She also noticed that Henrietta looked pale. "Why don't you two go across to the café and have a cup of coffee," she suggested. "I can handle things here for a while."

"Wonderful idea," Henrietta responded. "I could use a shot of caffeine."

"And perhaps a small sugar fix?" Ruth added mischievously, remembering her younger days when she would run across the street to the café and bring back delicious pastries while Henrietta made fresh coffee. But then a more serious look crossed her face as she said, "Are you sure this is okay, Sarah? I'm sure Tessa will be here any minute."

"Of course, it is. I'll be fine."

"If she's not here when I get back," Ruth said, "I'll call her cell again. There was no answer earlier, and she's probably on the road and hasn't noticed my message."

Several groups of quilters stopped at the booth while Ruth was gone, but Sarah was able to answer their questions and ring up their purchases. She was reminded how much she enjoyed retail, having worked for many years at Keller's Market before the children were born and again after their father died. Sarah didn't see herself as outgoing, but she enjoyed helping people figure out what they were looking for whether it was an ingredient in a recipe or a fabric for a pattern. She surprised herself when she realized she knew a lot more about quilting than she had realized.

When she saw Ruth returning alone, she asked about Henrietta. "Her daughter called and suggested that they get a wheelchair and stroll through the show before it gets busy. They invited me to join them, but I wanted to get back."

"You could have gone," Sarah assured her. "I've been getting along just fine."

Ruth thumbed through the credit card receipts and responded, "You certainly have!" About that time, a petite woman in her early forties came limping toward the booth calling out her apologies. Her right arm was in a sling.

"Tessa, what happened to you?" Ruth said as she carefully hugged the newcomer and turned toward Sarah. "Sarah, I want you to meet my dear friend, Tessa."

"I've heard so much about you," Sarah responded, extending her hand, but then pulled it back when she realized the woman had her purse in one hand and a sling on the other.

"I hope she told you I'm usually more dependable than this."

"Tessa, tell us what happened," Ruth repeated. "Are you okay?"

"There was an accident on the interstate early this morning. I had just stopped when I was rear-ended by this kid who had been on his cell phone. I was slammed into the car in front of me and my airbag slammed into me. The medics fixed me up with this contraption and offered to take me to the hospital, but I'm fine. It's probably just a sprain. They said nothing seemed to be broken." Turning to Ruth, she again apologized. "I'm so sorry, Ruth."

"There's nothing to apologize for, Tessa. I'm just glad you weren't hurt any more seriously. Are you sure you want to stay? Why don't you just walk through the show and go on home."

"Absolutely not! I've looked forward to this all month. Now, show me around the booth."

They had left one of the side tables empty for Tessa's kits, and she seemed pleased with the arrangement.

"I'll run out to the car and get the kits," Tessa said as she slipped her good arm into her jacket.

"No you won't," Ruth responded. "Just grab your keys and I'll follow you to your car. Sarah, can you manage here okay?"

"Of course," she replied. "Take your time. In fact, I'll bet Tessa could use a cup of coffee."

"Good idea. We'll make a quick stop at the café. Call me on my cell if you have any problems." When they returned, Sarah helped Tessa get unpacked, and her kits pleasingly displayed. Tessa seemed to be doing fine with one arm and was even able to ring up her customers with just a little help getting things into the shopping bags.

The three women had a steady stream of customers throughout the morning, and around noon, Sarah grabbed sandwiches and sodas for the three of them. "There are tables set up by the food vendors if you two want to take a break. I'll stay with the booth."

"Isn't it about time for your class?"

"I've decided to skip this first class," Sarah responded.

"Why would you do that?" Ruth replied frowning. "Isn't that the class on paper piecing? You were looking forward it."

"I don't want to leave you two. It looks to me like a lot more quilters have arrived. One of the vendors told me there were a half dozen buses unloading out front."

"We might get busy, but we'll just take one customer at a time. We can handle this, Sarah, and actually, it's to my advantage for you to take this class."

"How's that?" Sarah asked with an eyebrow raised.

"You said you wanted to learn paper piecing so that you could teach it at the shop, and I think that's a fantastic idea. My customers will love it. So, you need to learn how to do it," Ruth said firmly. "And besides," she added in a playful tone, "it's already paid for, and I can't write it off if you don't go."

"Okay, I'm convinced," Sarah chuckled. "I'll go, but I'll check with you two later and see how it's going." She reached under the table for her purse and tote bag containing her class materials. "

* * * * *

After the class, Sarah took a shortcut across the showroom to get back to Ruth's booth. She tried to do it without looking right or left, but she found tunnel vision to be impossible when walking down aisles where quilts were pleading for her attention from all sides. She was able to keep moving most of the time, but occasionally one reached out and grabbed her and insisted she stop.

She did come to a complete stop when she saw the sign about an Alzheimer's exhibit in one of the side rooms. According to the sign, the exhibit featured twenty-three quilts, mostly wall hangings, made by a local group of caregivers. Sarah paused to read the sign, and wondered if she should go ahead and see the exhibit, but she decided that the quilts deserved more than a cursory look, and she vowed to set aside a block of time and return the next day. She picked up a couple of brochures for Ruth and Tessa.

Arriving back at the Running Stitches booth, Sarah was shocked by the number of customers milling around. *I knew I shouldn't have left*, she admonished herself, as she hurried toward the booth. There were at least a half-dozen women waiting by the cash register, and several others were lined up at the cutting table. Tessa was helping a customer choose fat quarters for a class project, and Ruth had obviously just finished cutting a piece of fabric and was listing the charges on a piece of paper that she handed to her customer with a friendly smile.

How can she look so relaxed? Sarah marveled as she headed straight for the cash register, smiled her apologies to the women who were waiting, and began ringing up orders and processing payments.

Once they had caught up with the customers who had been waiting, Ruth began straightening up the cutting table while Sarah and Tessa talked with the few remaining customers. Sarah was able to answer most of their questions and turned to Ruth or Tessa for help when she needed it. Ruth was returning the bolts to the fabric table and tidying up the fat quarter baskets, which had been emptied by people searching for particular colors.

When the last customer left, Sarah asked, "So, how are you doing, Tessa? Is your arm hurting?"

"I'm doing just fine. I'll admit that I considered turning around and going home after the accident, but I'm so glad I didn't. I love being here and I'm looking forward to taking in the show when we slow down."

"I'd be happy to take care of the booth this afternoon. Why don't you both take a look around? There are some wonderful quilts on display."

"This was supposed to be your time to relax and have fun," Ruth objected, but realizing that Sarah seemed to enjoy working at the booth, she added, "Perhaps Tessa and

I will take you up on that offer later in the afternoon or tomorrow. How was your class?"

"Fantastic." Sarah reached into her project bag and pulled out her nearly finished sixteen-point Advent Star. "Paper piecing is a miracle," she announced as she spread her four blocks out on the cutting table. "I never could have gotten these points so perfect on my own."

"Oh my," Ruth exclaimed. She examined the blocks carefully and shook her head. "Neither could I, at least not in the few hours you were in class." The blocks each had four long, slender overlapping spikes. Once the four blocks were sewn together, the sections would form a sixteen-pointed star.

"And, you're practically finished."

"I know," Sarah responded excitedly. "This process makes it possible to create very intricate patterns in a short time. I think your customers will love it."

At the end of the day, as the doors were closing and the last customers had left, Ruth and Sarah began tidying up the booth for the next morning while Tessa checked into her room. "Saturdays can get pretty hectic," Ruth said as she replaced a bolt of batik. "Sunday afternoons, too," she added. "I sure hope Tessa can work without too much pain. You have classes scheduled on both days, don't you?"

"I do, but I thought that perhaps you could get your money back if you talk to the instructor before the class. There might even be a waiting list."

"I don't want to do that, Sarah. If Tessa seems to be in too much discomfort, I might be able to get Henrietta to help out for the few hours you'll be gone."

"Standing would be hard for her...."

"I thought of that, but she could sit and collect money and run credit cards, and she could always answer questions and make fabric suggestions. She's great at that."

"She just might enjoy it," Sarah responded, realizing too that it would give Ruth time with her old friend. "Okay, let's put that down as Plan B."

"What's Plan A?" Ruth asked, looking perplexed.

"You'll agree that I should cancel my classes and stay here and help."

"Plan A isn't going to happen. I'm looking forward to offering these new classes at the shop."

Chapter 5

The next morning the three women had agreed to meet in the coffee shop for breakfast before the show opened. Sarah and Ruth arrived first and had found seats overlooking the lake. "It looks more like the ocean," Sarah commented. She hadn't had a chance to enjoy the view since their rooms were on the front side of the hotel.

"Hi, girls," they heard someone say and looked up to see Tessa heading for the table without her sling and looking bright and cheerful. "What a beautiful day," she added as she pulled out a chair and sat down.

"Where's your sling?" Ruth asked with a frown.

"I have it in my tote bag just in case I need it later, but I woke up this morning feeling just fine.

"You're sure it's okay to have it off?"

"The young man who put it on said I might not need it. He was just being cautious."

"Didn't he tell you to go to the hospital?"

"Again," Tessa responded. "Caution. He had other folks to take care of, and he just wanted to make sure someone was going to check me out more thoroughly, but you know how it is. By our age," she said looking at Ruth, "we know our bodies. I'm just fine. Now, what are we ordering?"

Once breakfast was served, Sarah asked Tessa about her shop. "How did you get started?"

"Well, let's see. I'll start from the beginning. About eight years ago, my husband and I bought the shop. He was older than I and was retired and wanted to work with me in the shop. Unfortunately, he died not long after we bought the shop. ..."

"Oh, I'm sorry," Sarah responded.

Tessa smiled and nodded, but continued. "I sold our house and moved into the apartment above the shop."

"The apartment is cute," Ruth interjected. "She has antique furniture and quilts everywhere: hanging on the walls, stacked by the fireplace. She even uses a quilt as a table cloth."

"You have a fireplace in your apartment above the shop?" Sarah asked with surprise. She'd been picturing a small downtown shop, and a fireplace seemed unlikely.

"Yes, the shop is an end unit, and there's a fireplace downstairs as well."

Ruth spoke up again. "She has a wing-back chair on either side of the fireplace in the shop where customers can sit and enjoy the warmth. It's a lovely shop. We should take a field trip there some time—maybe our Friday night group would like to go too."

After breakfast, the three headed for the booth and removed the sheets they had spread over the merchandise. They were almost too busy the rest of the morning to even think about Tessa's arm. In fact, they accidentally worked right through Sarah's class.

"Have you girls had a chance to see the show yet?" Tessa asked once things slowed down, and they had grabbed a quick lunch.

"No," they answered in unison, "but …"

"Why don't you two walk around now? Sarah's already missed her class, and things have slowed down. Besides, I owe you something for being so patient with me yesterday."

Ruth started to object, but her friend stopped her and said, "Just go. Things will be fine here, and if there's a problem, I'll call you. Turn your phone on."

Moving a little faster than they would have liked, Sarah and Ruth managed to see most of the quilts and were able to stop at a few to examine them more closely. "This is not my favorite way to see a show," Ruth had commented, "but I've snapped at least two dozen pictures so we can sit down when we get home and look in more detail."

"I have pictures too," Sarah responded, "and Charles has a gadget for projecting them. We could take the quilt show to our Friday night group."

"Oh, that's a fantastic idea."

Sarah looked at her watch and said, "It's almost 3:00. I think I'll head back to the booth and see how Tessa's doing. You need to walk around and see the vendors. I'm sure you know many of them."

"How thoughtful, Sarah. I'd love to do that, and I wanted to see Henrietta and her daughter. I'll see you in an hour or so."

"Take your time."

Ruth waved her away and decided to take a few more pictures to add to their collection before visiting the other vendors.

An hour later, she came rushing back to the booth breathless with excitement and announced, "You won't believe what I have." Ruth reached into her bag and pulled out a small quilt covered with objects: a pocket with a stuffed animal, a zipper, colorful yarn, beads, and several decorative pieces like rick rack and buttons.

"What is this?" Sarah asked, looking confused. "A child's quilt?"

"No," Ruth responded excitedly. "It's called a fidget quilt. It's for people with Alzheimer's or actually any form of dementia. The vendor that makes them said that hers were designed by a geriatric nurse who wanted to offer her restless Alzheimer's patients something to see and feel—something to fiddle with."

"I love it," Sarah responded as she pulled the little stuffed bear out of the pocket, and discovered it was secured by a string so it couldn't be dropped or misplaced. "What an excellent idea."

"The vendor said they are becoming very popular and that quilters, in particular, are getting involved making them. Don't you think our Friday night group would like to make them for our nursing home?"

"I think they'd be as excited as I am," Sarah responded. "These are incredible, and there are so many ideas...."

"What's going on?" Tessa had just finished with her customer and came to see what they were talking about. They showed her the quilt and explained how it was being used and she, too, wanted to get involved. "I've wanted to start up a quilting group at my shop," Tessa said, "and this just might be the perfect way to get started." She took a picture of the quilt and said she would put it in her next newsletter. "If I can get some of my customers to come into the shop to work on this, I just might be able to keep them for a regular group."

"That's exactly how I got started," Ruth responded. "I asked for help to make pillowcases for a local adolescent group home, and I still have three of those original volunteers in our group."

It was almost closing time, but a group of shoppers was heading for the booth, so the three friends turned away from the fidget quilt to help them. One of the women spotted the little quilt and asked about it, so Ruth went through her explanation again. She later told Sarah that the woman wanted to buy it for her mother, but Ruth sent her to the vendor who was selling them.

"What time is tomorrow's class?" Ruth asked as they were closing down for the day. "You're *not* going to miss that one!"

"It's in the morning at 10:00. It's a two-hour class on trapunto."

"Good," Ruth responded. "That sounds like another good class to offer to my customers. I know two or three women who are eager to learn something new."

The show had been closed for ten minutes when Sarah saw a woman hurrying toward their booth. "Hi, ladies," she said, a bit out of breath. "I'm trying to catch everyone before they leave. The loudspeaker went on the blink this afternoon, so we're trying to let everyone know. ..."

"Is something wrong?" Ruth asked looking apprehensive.

"Oh no. We just wanted everyone to know that we're keeping the Alzheimer's exhibit open from 6:00 to 8:00 this evening for the staff and vendors. We'll leave the side door unlocked, and you'll see a sign that says *Staff Only*. I hope to see you there," she added excitedly as she hurried on to the next booth.

"Let's do it," Sarah said, locking the cash box and sliding it into Ruth's tote bag. "I peeked into the room earlier, and it looks fascinating. They are mostly wall hangings, and they were made by people with Alzheimer's and by their caregivers."

"Wonderful. I had a chance to read the brochure you brought, but let's go upstairs and freshen up first. We have another half-hour before they open the exhibit, and I want to call Anna and see how things are going at the shop."

"I'll meet you gals down there later," Tessa said as they were heading for the elevator. "I have a couple of phone calls to make too."

* * * * *

When Sarah and Ruth entered the Alzheimer's exhibit hall later that evening, they were met by total silence, although there were several dozen women in the room. Sarah noticed one woman with tears running down her cheeks. Several were dabbing at their eyes. Without speaking, the two women stopped in front of a large poster that had been placed just inside the door. Sarah slipped on her reading glasses.

This exhibit was conceived by a local quilt club, which had been touched by Alzheimer's. Over the past few years, two of their past members had been diagnosed with the disease, while others in the club were currently caring for family members with various forms of dementia. Thinking it would be therapeutic, the caregivers were encouraged to make small quilts as a way of expressing feelings they were reluctant to verbalize. When a local caregiver support group learned of the project, several of its members asked to participate as well.

The success of the program lead to the idea that perhaps those suffering from dementia might also benefit from the exercise, and within a year, five or six women who had been quilters in their past were included in the effort. Often, with the help of club members, they began speaking their forgotten words with fabric and thread.

The resulting quilts were deeply touching. Some were bold and angular while others appeared as a mishmash of colors and design. Some seemed to speak of anger and loss while others seemed to express loneliness and fear. All caused a strong visceral reaction in the observer. All were deeply touching.

As they were completed, the club began to display the quilts on the walls of the church basement where they met, and it ultimately became obvious these revealing works of art should be shared with others. The show entitled "Silent Voices" was first presented at City Hall for the city's residents and has since been displayed in several local venues. We hope you enjoy the show. Please sign our guest book and leave your comments as you leave.

Sarah and Ruth stood silently for a moment, under-standing now why the room seemed to contain such emotion. They slowly walked around the room, stopping at each quilt and allowing themselves to feel what the artist must have been trying to say. Some using bright reds and oranges in sharp, exaggerated shapes seemed to be striking out with anger. Others with their muted shades and random shapes seemed to express sadness and confusion.

One wall hanging that was made by a caregiver consisted of Hourglass blocks, some precisely lined up row by row and others scattered about in disarray.

Most of the quilts were exhibited on the four walls of the room, but in the middle of the room, there was a tall frame displaying a bed quilt. The identification tag attached said it had been made by the members of the quilt club at the end of the project as a way of expressing their own emotions. Each had contributed one block, and there were no rules other than for size. Each block was fourteen inches square, and they were separated by sashing.

One woman had divided her block in half, one side being very structured with half-square triangles in strong colors. The other side was done in muted shades of similar colors, but the placement of the pieces was undefined and scattered, somewhat like a crazy quilt. Another had covered a black background with appliquéd tears.

Sarah was particularly fascinated by one that had a small pieced house in the middle of the block, and it was surrounded by three or four thin borders. The final border was a red and yellow zigzag pattern made of half-square triangles. She wondered about the message. To her, it seemed to reflect the quilter's desire to protect her own home from the ravaging effects of Alzheimer's. As with the rest of the exhibit, she realized the messages were very personal, and the observer would see their own interpretation.

Sarah noticed that Ruth seemed to be lost in one particular wall hanging. It, too, was a crazy quilt pattern, but using only solid colors. It gave the impression of an Amish quilt, and Sarah wondered if it was reminding her friend of her own Amish background and the family who had been lost to her after she chose to marry outside the community.

Tessa arrived as they were leaving the hall, and they agreed to meet in Ruth's room at 7:00 and go out to dinner.

Chapter 6

The next morning, Sarah and Tessa sat in the café, sipping coffee and planning their day while they waited for their breakfast. Ruth had gone out to the van to get the extra box of fat quarters she had brought just in case they ran low. She had asked Sarah to order her a short stack of pancakes and bacon. "I'm going to need the energy today," she had said with a chuckle as she was leaving.

The waitress returned shortly with their three meals, but Ruth had not yet returned. "I wonder what's keeping her," Tessa said as she looked toward the parking lot.

"She probably ran into someone she knows," Sarah responded as she dug into her omelet with gusto. "I'm not usually this hungry in the morning."

"It's the fresh air blowing in over the lake," Tessa responded, surreptitiously dunking her donut into her coffee cup. They had all three taken a brisk walk along the side of the lake before breakfast.

By the time they had finished their meal and a second cup of coffee, Sarah was becoming concerned. Ruth still hadn't returned. "I think we should check the parking lot," she suggested.

"Why don't you do that, and I'll run into the convention center and see if she's at the booth," Tessa responded.

"That's unlikely since she ordered breakfast, but take a look. I'll have the waitress pack up her food and meet you there."

Sarah signed the check with her room number and headed for the parking lot.

Ruth's van appeared undisturbed, and when Sarah looked inside, she saw the box of fat quarters sitting on the back seat. *She hasn't even been here*, Sarah thought. Realizing Ruth must have forgotten something and returned to the booth, Sarah hurried toward their booth, only to find Tessa standing there alone.

"Where do you suppose she went?" Sarah said as she arrived at the booth.

"They're opening the doors to the public is ten minutes," Tessa responded. "I'm sure she'll be back by then."

But she wasn't.

A group of women who had come into the show together was heading toward Ruth's booth. "Hi," the woman in the lead called out before reaching them. Sarah immediately recognized her as one of Ruth's customers. Several of the other women in the group looked familiar as well. "Where's Ruth? We told her we'd be here bright and early."

"She had to step away, but I'm sure she'll be right back," Sarah responded. "Feel free to look around and let me know if you need any help." Turning to Tessa, she quietly asked her to try Ruth's cell phone.

"I think I recognize you from the shop," one of the women said to Sarah. "Don't you teach classes?"

"I do," Sarah responded. "In fact, I'm getting ready to take the trapunto class and hope to be offering it to Ruth's customers in the fall."

"I'm glad to hear that. I wanted to sign up for that class, but we're only here for a few hours, and I didn't want to give up any show or vendor-shopping time. By the way, I'm Linda."

"I'm glad to meet you, Linda. I'm Sarah." Looking past the woman for a moment, she saw Tessa closing her cell phone and shaking her head. She shrugged her shoulders, indicating that she got no answer.

Two of the other women in the group were looking at Tessa's kits, and the woman Sarah had been talking with was picking up a bolt which she laid on the cutting table. "Could I get two yards of this, please?"

"Tessa, I'll get this. You can help the women who are looking at your kits."

"Oh, these are yours?" one of the women said looking surprised. "I thought this was all Ruth's merchandise."

"Most of it is," Tessa explained. "I'm just here to help out, and Ruth said I could bring my kits. Here's a picture of that quilt finished," she added as she reached into her box under the table and pulled out a few pictures which she placed by the kits.

"These are lovely. And everything I need is in the package?"

"Everything except the back. You'll need four yards for that one."

"Maybe I should get it now. What do you think would look good with it?" Tessa quickly scanned across the bolts and reached for a tan and green paisley. Sarah saw Tessa grimace as she lifted the bolt, and she made a mental note to ask about her arm once the customers were gone.

"This would look nice," she offered, opening the kits and spreading the fabrics out for comparison."

"You have a good eye," the woman responded. "That's a perfect match. I'll take four yards."

As the women were leaving, Tessa suddenly said, "Sarah! Your class. Ruth will be disappointed if you miss another one."

"But she isn't back and …"

"Just go. Remember, I run a shop, and I'm accustomed to having groups of quilters arrive all at once. I can handle it."

"And your arm? You looked like you were in pain when you reached for that fabric earlier."

"It's nothing. I probably just pulled something. I can always put the sling on, and customers will be sympathetic and help out with the lifting. For now, I'm fine. Go!"

"If Ruth isn't back by the time I return, we need to do something."

"Like what?"

"I don't know. Maybe see if the loudspeaker has been fixed and have her paged."

"Go to class. I'll keep trying her cell phone, but I'm sure she'll be here by the time you get back."

Two hours later as Sarah was leaving the classroom, she heard an announcement over the loudspeaker that stopped her dead in her tracks.

"Ruth Weaver, please report to the Admissions Desk. Ruth Weaver. Report to the Admissions Desk."

Sarah hurried toward the booth wondering what had happened.

As she approached, she saw a small crowd of security people milling around. "I'm sorry, Sarah," Tessa said pleadingly as she left the booth to meet Sarah. "I just started getting scared. I talked to one of the security men, and he felt something should be done right away. I wanted to wait for you. ..."

"No, Tessa. You did the right thing. I was just assuming she'd be here when I got back. What have they said to you?"

"They've done a thorough search of the convention center and have been to our three rooms. They're waiting for the police now to do a search of the entire premises and the surrounding grounds. Oh, Sarah, what's happened to her?"

Sarah gave the petite woman a hug but couldn't find any words to offer her comfort. She fought to maintain control herself as she felt anxiety rushing throughout her body. Until that moment, she hadn't taken Ruth's disappearance seriously. She was sure her friend had just lost track of time—an easy thing to do at a quilt show.

"Has anyone called her husband?" Sarah asked.

"Should we?" Tessa responded. "I hate to scare him, but ..."

"I know, but maybe he's heard from her."

"Good thought," Tessa replied. "Do you have his number?"

"Yes. I'll do it."

As she spoke, a few uniformed policemen entered the room and appeared to be chatting with the security people. *And I'll call my husband as well*, Sarah reassured herself.

* * * * *

"So, what did the police have to say?" Charles asked patiently, trying to help his wife calm down.

"They looked around, and they took what little information Tessa and I had. They took her husband's phone number and said they would be calling him, and that I should wait to contact him until after they had spoken with him. Despite all that, I just have the feeling that they aren't taking this very seriously."

"I can understand that," Charles, a retired detective himself, responded. "She's only been gone a few hours, and adults have the right to simply walk away whenever they want and stay gone for as long as they want. Without evidence of something suspicious, it's really not a police matter."

"Well, it should be, Charles. She didn't just walk off—she left her breakfast to get a box of fabric from the car, and she never came back. If that isn't suspicious behavior, I don't know what is."

Her voice had risen a few octaves as she talked, and Charles realized his words weren't offering her any solace. *My lifetime of being a cop just comes out when I least expect it*, he admonished himself. "I'll leave now and get there as quickly as I can," Charles responded.

She hated for him to come running to her side yet again. It seemed he was always having to give her support. *How did I get along before he was in my life?* she asked herself. But she could immediately answer her own question. Before she met Charles, her life was very simple. Busy, but simple. After Jonathan died, she was either working at Keller's Market or working in her garden.

Since moving to Cunningham Village, Sarah had branched out into the world of activities, people, and education. She was now comfortable in cyberspace, had learned to quilt, was teaching classes, and traveling to quilt retreats. She had developed a loving relationship with a man, had close friends, and still had the time to enjoy her family. With all that, there had been occasional complications that she hadn't experienced in her previous life, but she felt much better off than some of the older people she knew in the village who spent their days simply waiting to die.

"Thank you, Charles. I appreciate that. Call me on my cell phone when you get here. I'll let the desk know you'll need a key."

"Okay, sweetie, and let them know you'll be staying at least another day. I'll see you in a few hours."

As she was closing her phone, a pleasant looking man in a suit and tie approached her. "Mrs. Parker?"

"Yes?"

"I'm Detective Krakowski. Could we go somewhere and talk? I understand you know Mrs. Weaver very well."

"Sure, Detective Kra …"

"Krakowski," he repeated. "Jake Krakowski. How about the coffee shop?"

"Fine," she responded. "First I need to speak with Tessa. I think we should just close the booth."

"I agree."

Sarah suggested that Tessa cover the merchandise with the sheets that Ruth had stored under the table. "And if you don't mind sitting in the booth until I get back, just to keep her things safe."

"Of course, Sarah. I'll be right here."

Turning to the detective, Sarah asked if they had contacted Ruth's husband. He said they had and that he was on his way. They left the convention center, and the detective led her to a table in the far corner of the coffee shop where they could talk. The center and particularly the area around Ruth's booth had become very chaotic with security people, policemen, and curious bystanders.

"There's been a development," Jake Krakowski began. Sarah looked at him with trepidation.

"What?" she asked, barely wanting to hear his response.

"We found her purse in the parking lot. Nothing appears to be missing. Her wallet is there with cash and credit cards. Her cell phone is there …"

Sarah's heart sank. Ruth wouldn't be calling her.

"… and this suggests the possibility that she left here against her will."

"Kidnapped?" Sarah gasped. "You think she was kidnapped?"

"Not necessarily but it's a possibility, Mrs. Parker. Do you have any idea who she might have left with?"

"Absolutely not. Ruth Weaver is a kind, loving friend and …" Her voice cracked, and she reached for a napkin. She remained quiet until she regained her composure. "Who would do this?" she asked, not expecting an answer.

"What do you know about her? Does she have family?"

"There's her husband, Nathan, of course. And she has a daughter working in Kentucky.…" She gasped again. "Someone needs to call her.…"

"Her husband will take care of that," the detective said calmly.

"Of course. Her sister and her brother-in-law live near her, and they're managing her shop while she's away.…" Again her voice cracked, but she continued to maintain control of her emotions.

"Parents? Siblings?"

"Ruth was Amish. She married outside the faith and was no longer welcome in her community. Her parents are dead now, and she doesn't see her Amish siblings, except for Anna, who also left the sect."

"Would anyone from her community be behind this?"

"She been gone for many years, detective, and she's from a peaceful community. There'd be no reason for them to hurt her. No, it's someone else, but I have no idea who. Maybe Nathan or her sister Anna will have an idea. ..."

They sat for another twenty minutes or so while Sarah ran through everything that Ruth had done since arriving at the show.

"You were in separate rooms," he began, "so you don't know what she did during the evenings I guess. Could she have been meeting someone?"

Is he suggesting she might have been having an affair? Sarah wondered. "I can't vouch for her for her whereabouts in the evenings ... well, except for Saturday night when we went to the Alzheimer's Exhibit and a late dinner, but," she continued with growing irritation in her voice, "I think what you're suggesting is absurd. She's ..."

"Mrs. Parker, I'm not suggesting anything, I assure you. We have no theories other than to suspect that she may not have left willingly. Please understand that we must ask questions in order to eliminate all possibilities."

"I know," she muttered, dropping her eyes. "I know. I'm just so worried. ..."

They sat quietly while Sarah composed herself. He then reached for his briefcase, thanked her for her help, and as he stood he handed her his card. "Call me if you think of anything else."

As he walked away, she looked down at the card in her hand: Detective Jake Krakowski. Jake, she remembered he had said. *A nice man like Charles*, she thought. *A gentle man.* She wondered how men like Jake and Charles could survive the things they had to deal with in their jobs. She slipped the card into her pocket and slowly walked back to the convention center.

It was early afternoon, and the police were making an exhaustive search of the facility. Many of the guests were spending more time speculating about what might be going on than they were spending time at the show. Several announcements were made to assure people that there was no danger and that the show would remain open until 5:00, the scheduled closing time.

Tessa and Sarah decided that they would shut down Ruth's booth under the circumstances. As they began packing, the two young men that Ruth had hired previously appeared at the booth. "We thought you might be leaving," the older one said. "We heard what happened. Have they found that lady yet?"

"No, not yet, but I'm glad you thought to come by. I was wondering how to reach you. Let's go ahead and pack up." She suddenly remembered that the trailer and the van were both locked, and Ruth had the key. "Oh, wait," she exclaimed. "We can't get into the trailer."

"Didn't you say that detective found her purse? Maybe he has the keys," Tessa suggested.

"Your right," Sarah responded. "I'll go find him." She approached the first police officer she came to and pulled the card out of her pocket. "Could you page Detective Krakowski and tell him I need to speak with him. I'm Sarah Parker." Moments later he appeared at her side. "You must have been nearby," she exclaimed.

"Actually, I was on my way over here to meet Mrs. Weaver's husband. He just called to say he was on his way into the building. What can I do for you?"

"I wanted to ask about her keys. We need to get into the trailer, but if Nathan is here, he'll have the key."

At that moment, Nathan came running up and grabbed Sarah's arm. Detective Krakowski stepped forward protectively. "What's going on Sarah," Nathan pleaded. "What's happened to my wife?"

Sarah nodded reassuringly to the detective letting him know it was okay as she wrapped her arms around Nathan protectively. "Nathan, they'll find her. Everyone is searching. We have to stay strong for Ruth." Pulling away slightly, she turned toward the detective and introduced the two men. Nathan ran his fingers through his already mussed hair, looking confused and anxious.

"I'm sorry," Nathan said, trying to pull himself together. "I just … where is she?"

"Let's sit down and talk," Detective Krakowski said, pointing toward the chairs which the young men had moved to the side of the booth. Mrs. Parker, will you join us?"

"Please call me Sarah," she responded as she moved toward the two men.

"And Krakowski is a mouthful," the detective responded. "Just call me Jake. We're going to be spending a great deal of time together. Let's keep it simple," he added with a smile.

"You too Mr. Weaver," he added as he handed Nathan his card.

"Thank you, Jake. It's Nathan, and I'm sorry for the histrionics. I'm just terrified. What's happened to my wife?"

"That's what we're trying to find out."

The three sat and went over most of the same material that Jake and Sarah had discussed in the coffee shop. Nathan didn't have much to add since he'd only spoken with his wife twice since she left home. "She called me Friday night to let me know she got here safely, and again on Saturday night. It was sort of late when she called. She'd been somewhere with Sarah, I think?" he said, looking at Sarah questioningly.

"Yes, that's the night we went to the exhibit and then to dinner."

"Did you see her speak to anyone at the restaurant?"

"No. We were seated right away by the window overlooking the water."

"Where?"

"We walked up to that seafood restaurant a couple of blocks up the street.... I forget the name.... Scruffy's or something."

Jake smiled. "Scupper's," he responded. "I'll send someone down to see if they noticed anything unusual."

"It was the next morning that she disappeared, right?" Nathan asked. "Right after breakfast?"

Sarah explained how they had met for breakfast, but Ruth said she wanted to get a box of fat quarters out of the van. "She ordered pancakes and said she'd be right back."

"Is the box still in the van?"

"Yes, there's no evidence she ever made it to the van," Jake responded.

"Where did you find her purse?" Nathan's voice cracked on the last couple of words, and he dropped his eyes to hide the emotions which washed over him as he thought about his wife being taken.

"A few yards beyond the van."

"She walked past the van? Why would she do that?" Nathan stood and began pacing. "Nothing about this makes any sense," he exclaimed. Turning to the detective, he demanded, "What are you people doing to find her? Why are you sitting here with us when …"

"Nathan," Sarah interrupted. "The police force is out searching for her. Detective Krakowski is on our side."

"Sorry," Nathan muttered as he sat back down and buried his face in his hands. Sarah and Jake moved away and gave him privacy.

"I'm going back to the station and see if there's been any news. You have my card. Call me, Sarah."

"Thank you, Jake. I will."

"Is your husband coming? You shouldn't be alone."

"He's on his way," she responded with a weak smile. "We'll be heading home tomorrow."

He took her hand and looked into her eyes. "We'll find her, Sarah."

Such a kind man, she thought as she headed for the elevator and her room.

Chapter 7

"Are you sure we should be leaving?" Sarah asked, still not comfortable with leaving Chicago with her friend missing. They'd only been on the road for twenty minutes, and she was already thinking they should turn back.

"Jake said there's nothing we can do there, Sarah, and we're just a phone call away. He'll be in touch for sure."

"How can you be so sure?"

"Couldn't you tell?" Charles responded with a mischievous look on his face. "The guy's a little sweet on you."

"Charles! How can you say that? First of all, I'm old enough to be his mother. And second of all …"

"Relax, sweetie. I'm just teasing you, but he does think a lot of you. That was obvious."

"Well, I liked him too. He's very kind and sensitive for a detective."

"For a detective? And just what does that mean?"

Fearing that she had offended him, she glanced over but saw that he was grinning. "You know what I mean. I'm just glad he's in charge of the case. He'll find her, won't he?"

"I'm sure he will."

They drove silently for the next few miles. Sarah saw that her husband seemed to be lost in his thoughts. Finally she asked. "Where are you?"

"Wondering if there's any way I can help."

"Do you have any ideas?" she asked hopefully.

"Not yet, but I'm working on it. There's something that just doesn't feel right. I think I'll give Jake a call tomorrow."

When Charles arrived in Chicago the previous night, it was obvious that he and Jake had immediate rapport. The three had met in the evening for drinks and, while Sarah sat back quietly watching their growing comradery, the two men discussed Ruth's disappearance and their experiences with similar cases. They would occasionally glance at her and stop talking, and Sarah knew those were the cases with unpleasant outcomes. "You boys don't have to pussyfoot around with me," she had said at one point. "I'm realistic, and I know that this might not work out the way we all hope it will."

Jake had smiled and said to Charles, "that's some gal you have there."

"I know," he responded, winking at his wife. "I know."

* * * * *

The phone was ringing when they arrived home. "Let it go to the machine, Charles. I need to get settled in before I have to start telling this story to all our friends."

"I don't think you'll have much to tell. They already know," he said as he laid the open newspaper in front of her. "Local woman missing. Authorities suspect foul play."

Sarah, still wearing her jacket, grabbed the paper and sat down to read it. "Oh, Charles, this is terrible. Look what they say here. . . ."

Charles took the paper and quickly scanned the article. "This is just your usual sensationalism, Sarah. We were there! We know this isn't how Jake sees the case." According to the paper, circumstances of her disappearance were suspicious, and the article made it sound like her husband was the prime suspect. "It would probably help," Charles began, "if the departments weren't always so secretive about their investigations. That just leads to reporters speculating and what they come up with is usually worse than the facts."

"But Charles, I think we should call Nathan and make sure he's okay."

"We can do that, and I'm planning to call Jake as soon as we get settled. Right now I'm going to walk over to Andy's house to pick up Barney."

After Charles had left, Sarah sat down to play the messages. Two were from Sophie, and the rest were from members of the Friday night quilting group. She didn't think she had the energy to tell the story over and over, so she decided to call Sophie and get the phone tree going and invite everyone to an emergency meeting at the shop. She called Anna first to make sure it was okay with her since she was running the shop.

Anna's husband Geoff answered the phone and said Anna was at the shop. "She's planning to close early so she can be home when Katie arrives." Katie, Ruth's daughter, was working in Paducah at the quilt museum and was on her way home to be with the family.

"How's Anna holding up?" Sarah asked.

"She's worried about her sister of course, but that woman is a real trouper. She just keeps going. I think it's her Amish background. She holds back her emotions and just keeps going."

"I'll call her at the shop and see how she feels about an emergency meeting of the quilters."

"I think she'll be pleased with that, Sarah. They've all been calling her night and day to ask about Ruth. She'll be glad to have you explain exactly what's happening."

"Is there anything I can do to help her?" Sarah asked. "Maybe help out at the shop?"

"I think Katie will be working with her, but ask when you call. The more people she has around her, the better."

As Sarah hung up, the front door swung open, and Barney came leaping across the floor toward her. All efforts to remind him about jumping up on people failed and Sarah finally sat down and let him climb onto her lap and smother her with kisses. "You're too big to be up here, fellow," she said laughing as she scratched both of his ears at once. "I missed you, too."

"Andy said Caitlyn is going to be lost without Barney. He's been sleeping stretched out across the bottom of her bed. Andy's beginning to wonder whether it might be time to make a trip to the shelter."

"A dog for Caitlyn? Oh, Charles! That would be wonderful. She's so good with Barney and Emma. I hope they do it."

"Did you get the meeting set up for tonight?"

"I'm getting ready to call Anna now. I spoke with Geoff, and he said Katie is on her way."

Charles and Barney went into the kitchen and left Sarah to make her calls. Anna agreed that a meeting was exactly what everyone needed. "They have so many questions that I can't answer," she had said. Anna offered to get the phone tree going so that everyone would get a personal call about the meeting.

After she hung up, she got her cell phone out and moved into the bedroom so she could rest while she talked to Sophie. She and Sophie had been talking over the past two days from Chicago and even during the drive home that morning, but Sarah wanted to tell her about the meeting personally.

"Aren't you too tired to go out?" Sophie asked.

"I'm tired, but it's easier than making all those phone calls. Anyway, I think her friends need to get together for support."

"You're right. I know I sure need it. I'll pick you up around 7:00," Sophie offered, knowing her friend would be exhausted by evening. Sarah hung up and immediately fell into a deep sleep.

She awoke suddenly over an hour later when she felt a tiny warm and scratchy tongue on her hand. "Boots! Hello there. Did you miss me too?" Boots began purring and rubbing against Sarah. "Is this love or hunger?" Sarah asked as she reached for her slippers.

"Do you feel better?" Charles asked when she walked into the kitchen. There was a pot simmering on the stove.

"What have you made?" she asked, surprised to find him cooking.

"I made a hearty soup for our dinner," he responded, pushing his chest out with pride. "I think you'll like it."

Sarah looked into the pot and saw meat and vegetables swimming in a thick bubbling broth. "This smells wonderful." It wasn't until later that she chuckled when she spotted two large cans in the recycle bin labeled hearty beef vegetable soup.

At precisely 7:00, Sarah heard Sophie pull into the driveway. She was putting on her jacket when there was a knock at the door. Sarah opened it, and Caitlyn burst in full of excitement and talking without taking a breath. "Daddy told you about my dog, right? Isn't it wonderful? I can hardly wait. Will you go with us when we go to look? I think I want a big dog or maybe a small one. I don't know. I'll just have to look. What do you think, Sarah? Should I get a very young dog so I can train him from the beginning? I wonder how Barney will feel about this. ..."

"Whew," Charles said laughing. "Take a breath, young lady."

Caitlyn looked at Sarah and saw the sadness in her eyes and her excitement quickly faded. "I'm sorry. I shouldn't be so excited when your friend is missing. I'm sorry, Sarah."

Sarah smiled and put her arm around the young girl's shoulder. "You don't have anything to be sorry about, Caitlyn. Of course, you're excited about getting a dog, and I would be too, and even Ruth would understand. And yes, I'd love to go with you when you go."

"How did you decide on Barney? Were there lots of dogs there when you went to the shelter?"

"There were. And I had no idea how I would decide, but as it turned out there was no problem at all. The moment I looked into Barney's eyes, we both knew. And if that doesn't happen for you, then we just go home, and we go back another day. I promise that your dog is out there, and you'll know it when you meet him or her. Just wait." Caitlyn saw some of Sarah's sparkle return to her eyes as she talked about the dog.

Sophie leaned on her horn reminding them that she was ready to go, and they both knew she was not fond of waiting. Sarah kissed Charles on the cheek, and the two hurried out to the car.

When they arrived at the shop, Anna was watching for them and unlocked the door. Anna's eyes were red and swollen, and the room was silent despite there being seven or eight members already there. As Sarah looked around, she was surprised to see several members who hadn't been to the meetings for months.

"Myrtle," she said softly. "I'm so glad to see you." Myrtle was in her eighties and hadn't been to a meeting for over a year, although she occasionally came into the store and was very fond of Ruth.

Sarah looked around and smiled when she saw Frank, who had been their only male member. She went over and spoke with him as well. She then nodded at Allison, who was whispering with Delores. Christina and Kimberly sat together and looked very somber.

"We're glad you're here, Sarah," Anna said. "Come sit up here in the front so everyone can see you while you're speaking." Sarah hadn't realized she would be leading the meeting, but as she quickly contemplated this, she realized it made sense. She was the only one who knew what had happened and could answer some of their questions. Unfortunately, she knew there was much she couldn't help them with. No one knew what had happened to Ruth.

"Okay," she responded as she moved to the chair Anna had placed in front of the group. "I read the articles in the paper, and I'd like to straighten out some of the misconceptions presented there. First and foremost, I want everyone to know that Nathan is *not* a suspect. He has remained in Chicago to be available to the police if he's needed. I think it's very likely that my husband will be joining him as well. You all know Charles is a retired detective himself. I guess another thing I'd like everyone to know is that the detective investigating this case seems to be a very kind and sensitive man, and I think he'll find out what happened to our friend. He seems determined to do just that."

She looked around the room at Ruth's friends and saw the pain and sadness on their faces. She didn't know what she could say to help. She felt just like they did. "Tell me what questions you have that I might be able to answer," she asked.

"Can you tell us how she disappeared? Did anyone see her leave?" Delores asked.

Sarah started from the beginning, as she did with Detective Krakowski, and told them briefly about the two days before and then went into detail about the morning she disappeared. She talked about the detective and his questions and about Nathan's arrival. She was hesitant to mention the fact that they found her purse, but she decided to give them all the information she had. They loved Ruth too.

"Well, if her purse was tossed aside, maybe it was a robbery, but then they probably wouldn't have taken her. ..."

"It was not a robbery," Sarah said sadly. "Nothing was missing from the purse."

"Then why ..." and the speaker stopped and gasped. "You mean they wanted her specifically?"

"But why?"

"What did the detective say about the purse?"

"Was she kidnapped?" Allison asked incredulously?

"The detective said that is a possibility," Sarah responded unable to keep up with the questions being fired her way.

"But why?" someone repeated.

"No one knows," she responded.

"Are there any clues?" Frank asked. Frank was mentally challenged but high functioning. He had a job and loved detective stories. He originally stopped by the shop to ask about lessons so he could make a quilt for his grandmother. Sarah smiled at his question and stood up to answer him.

"I'm sure there are, Frank. But you know how the police are with their clues. They keep them to themselves while they investigate."

They asked a few more questions, expressed some opinions, and then began talking about their own feelings, including what Ruth had meant to them. Sarah realized it was beginning to sound like a memorial service, and she immediately turned it around, not wanting to think she was gone forever.

"There's something else I wanted to tell you about the show in Chicago. Ruth and I took dozens of pictures of the quilts, and we plan to use my husband's projector and bring the Chicago show to our meeting just as soon as Ruth returns. Everyone stopped talking and stared at her for a few seconds.

Sarah continued, "Ruth is very excited about sharing the show with her friends and particularly the Alzheimer's

Exhibit so we'll all be looking forward to that." She stood up again and added, "Now let's dig into those refreshments and start making plans for our next few meetings."

As people stood and moved toward the refreshment table, Sarah noticed a slight change in their demeanor. She heard Kimberly laugh at something her sister said, and Frank was asking Myrtle about the quilt she had in her tote bag. Myrtle pieced by hand and took her projects wherever she went. She proudly spread it out on a nearby table for Frank to see and Caitlyn joined them.

Sophie, realizing what Sarah had done, winked at her and mouthed, "Well done."

The meeting broke up early so Anna could get home to her niece, Ruth's daughter, Katie, who had arrived that afternoon. Katie had been working at the quilt museum in Paducah since her graduation from art school the previous year. Anna told Sarah privately that Katie wanted to drive up to Chicago to be with her father, but Nathan had discouraged it and asked her to stay and help Anna in the shop. "This is no place for my daughter," Nathan had said to Anna, "and I don't want her to see me like this."

"I wish he'd just come home. I'm sure there's nothing he can do there," Anna said.

"Charles is thinking about going up and offering his help. Maybe he can convince Nathan to allow him to take his place. He should be here for Katie."

"Good idea, Sarah. Let me know if he decides to do that. We all need Nathan back here."

Sophie drove Caitlyn home first and slowed down in front of her own house. "It's still early. Would you like to come in for a cup of coffee?"

"It's been a long trying day, Sophie, physically and emotionally. I just want to go home and sleep. How about you come to my house in the morning, and we'll have brunch. Also, I have something I want to show you."

"Okay, that's a better plan. I want to talk to you about my appliqué project, and we'll be more relaxed in the morning. I made a batch of oatmeal cookies this morning, and I'll bring what's left."

Sophie dropped Sarah off at her door and said, "See you about 10:00?"

"Perfect!" Sarah replied, already thinking about spending many hours in her own bed.

Chapter 8

The next morning, Sophie arrived right on time. Sarah was taking the breakfast casserole out of the oven, coffee was brewing, and the table was set for two. "What about Charles?" Sophie asked.

"He got up long before I did, ate breakfast, and retired to his den to pay bills, file some insurance claims, and play around on his computer. He said he was going to leave us alone so we could have 'girl time,' as he called it.

"We need it," Sophie responding pouring herself a cup of coffee and loading it up with cream and sugar. "What's in this casserole?"

"Many wonderful things: cheese, ham, eggs, mushrooms, onions, peppers, …"

"Yum!" Sophie respond, grabbing the serving spoon and filling her plate. Sarah pulled a pan of biscuits out of the oven and slid them into the bread basket.

"Orange juice?"

"Love some, and maybe some butter and jelly?"

"It's on the way."

Moments later, Sarah joined her friend at the table, and they spent the next hour eating, laughing, and catching up on all the happenings while Sarah was away. But neither woman mentioned Ruth. They seemed to realize that Sarah needed a brief break from the worry."

After they finished eating and straightened up the kitchen, they moved into the living room. "I'd like to talk to you about my quilt project," Sophie said as she sat down and placed her tote bag on the couch." Barney came over and sniffed the bag, but seemed to have decided it wasn't promising. He sighed and laid across Sophie's feet.

"And there's something I wanted to show you," Sarah responded as she sat down next to Sophie.

Sophie started to reach into her bag, but hesitated and said, "I think I'd like for you to go first." She noticed that Sarah also had a tote bag, and her curiosity was getting the better of her.

"Okay." She then told Sophie about the fidget quilts and how they were used with people suffering from dementia. She reached into her tote bag and pulled out the one Ruth had purchased at the show.

"This is incredible," Sophie exclaimed as she ran her hand over the various textures. She squeezed the small, stuffed animal and was delighted to hear it squeak. "My husband would have loved this," she added, as a cloud of grief passed briefly across her face. Her husband had died in the nursing home several years before. He had suffered the ravages of Alzheimer's, and Sophie had suffered the loss of her husband, bit by bit. During the last six months of his life, he didn't even recognize her. She was rarely able to talk about it.

Brightening up, she added, "You know, we could make these for those folks at the nursing home."

"Exactly. I thought about mentioning it at the meeting last night, but I decided to wait until Ruth is back. She was very excited about the idea."

"Good decision," Sophie responded. "Let's wait a few weeks. Now, let's get to my question." Sophie reached into her tote and pulled out the appliquéd blocks she had completed. "Aren't these pretty?" she stated, as she gently placed three blocks on the coffee table,

"They're beautiful, Sophie. I knew you'd be good at this. Your embroidery work was always flawless, and I was sure you'd be good at appliqué."

"You're embarrassing me," Sophie responded, brushing Sarah's words away with the wave of her hand. "But let's talk about putting them together in a quilt."

"We can't do that until you get them all appliquéd...." Sarah began, but Sophie immediately interrupted her.

"I know, I know, but I'm just trying to understand what we'll be doing. I don't get how this will become a quilt."

"Okay, let's look at the picture on the front of the kit." Sophie pulled it out along with the fabric included.

"See, these pale green strips will go between your appliquéd blocks like this." Sarah pointed to the sashing in the picture. "And that same fabric will go all the way around the finished blocks making an inner border." She pulled out the small pieces of assorted pastels. "These will be used to make the stars in the sashing—those are called cornerstones."

"And you'll do all those?"

"Absolutely. In fact, I've been thinking about starting on the cornerstones, so they'll be ready when you are."

"Then this must be the border?" Sophie said, holding up a piece of fabric in several shades of green.

"Yes, that will be the final border and binding."

"What about the back?"

"Most kits come without backs, and we'll go shopping for that once we're finished. You can pick out whatever you like."

"How will I know what to like?" Sophie asked with a worried look.

Sarah laughed. "You'll know, and if you don't, Ruth and I will help. It's going to be beautiful."

"You did it again."

"Did what?" Sarah responded.

"You referred to Ruth as if you think she'll be back with us one day."

"I absolutely believe that, Sophie."

"You really do?"

"Yes, I do."

"Okay, then so do I."

"Good. Now let's have another cup of coffee and talk about what we're going to do this afternoon. I need an outing."

"Okay, but let me put my blocks away first. I'm so afraid I'll spill something on them."

"It's good to be careful, but remember that you're using cotton—it's washable."

"Oh no," Sophie exclaimed, pulling her blocks close to her heart protectively.

"I remember being like that with my first quilt," Sarah chuckled. "Now I stuff them in the washing machine and push the button."

"Oh my," Sophie frowned. "I don't think ..." but her words trailed off as she saw Charles coming into the living room looking apprehensive.

"What is it?" Sarah asked, standing as she registered the look on her husband's face.

"I just got off the phone with Jake," he replied. "They've officially classified the case as a kidnapping."

"Oh no," Sarah responded, slipping back onto the chair. "I was hoping ..."

"Why would anyone kidnap a middle-aged quilt shop owner?" Sophie demanded impatiently. "How did they come up with this idea anyway?"

"A witness came forward," Charles responded. "The man lives in the condo across from the convention center, and he reported seeing a woman who appeared to be struggling with someone Sunday morning in the parking lot. He thought the whole thing looked suspicious, but when they drove away, he disregarded it."

"Why is this man just now telling someone about this?" Sarah asked. Her voice was raised with mounting anger, causing Barney to jump up and move over by her feet. She reached down and scratched his ear reassuringly, but turned back to Charles. "So, what took him so long?"

Charles walked over and laid his hand on her shoulder gently. "He's been out of town. According to Jake, the guy was heading for the airport that morning. He came out of his building and was getting into the cab when he noticed them. He told Jake he was concerned at first, but then they drove away, and he figured it was just a domestic dispute."

"Well, I think he should have done something right away."

"I know, Sarah, but sometimes we don't want to interfere in other people's business, and I'm sure he had other things on his mind. Jake said the guy called the police yesterday immediately after he returned and saw it in the newspaper."

Sarah looked resigned but muttered, "People should look out for each other. ..."

"It's a fine line," Charles responded. Hoping to lighten the mood, he turned to Sophie and asked about her dog.

"Emma's just a bundle of joy," Sophie responded with a wide grin. Emma was her first dog, and she was enjoying the many benefits. "She's always so happy to see me, even when I come back in the house from taking the garbage out. She acts like I've been gone for days."

"It's that unconditional love," Sarah added, stroking Barney's head that was now stretched out across her lap. "He knew I was upset a few minutes ago, and here he is trying to comfort me."

The three sat quietly for a while sipping coffee and munching on oatmeal cookies. Finally, Charles sighed and looked at his wife for a moment before speaking.

"I think I could be very helpful to the department if I did some legwork for them. I'll just bet there are other people who know something. They've interviewed the shopkeepers in the neighborhood, but I think that someone needs to look at their early morning sales that day and try to contact customers."

Once the words were out, he sat quietly, looking thoughtful. He had promised his wife that he wouldn't pursue police work again, *but perhaps this is different*, he thought.

Finally he added in a serious tone, "What do you think, Sarah?"

She sighed. "Promise me you won't put yourself in danger?"

He nodded his head slightly, knowing he couldn't make that promise. He knew he would follow any leads he found. Finally he said, "I'm always careful."

Sarah knew he was going to do it and loved him for caring enough to help her friend. "At least if you go, we can bargain with Nathan." He turned to her with a puzzled look.

"Let's tell him that you'll come up to Chicago and help with the investigation if he'll come home. Anna needs him and now his daughter, Katie, is here and begging to go to Chicago to be with him. He's needed at home."

"Okay, it's a deal. You call Nathan, and I'll leave tomorrow morning."

Chapter 9

Sarah took her seat at the worktable and greeted everyone. Most of the members had arrived early to participate in the fat quarter raffle they had planned for this week. Telephone calls and emails had been flying among the members, and it was ultimately decided that the Friday Night Quilters would continue to meet just as they had when Ruth was there. "It's what she would want," several members had said. This would be their first regular meeting without Ruth.

They got right to the raffle, skipping the usual formalities. No one wanted to bring up Ruth's absence just yet. Each member had agreed to bring in fat quarters to donate to the raffle. For each fat quarter a member brought in, that person got one chance to win all the fat quarters. Delores had brought the most, placing a dozen blue and yellow fat quarters into the large basket Anna had brought in from the store room. Anna gave her twelve chances.

Sarah brought five from her Civil War collection and Christina and Kimberly together contributed another ten. "I want to be in on this too," Anna said, grabbing her tote bag and placing another six on the growing pile.

"Here are my two," Allison offered.

"Wait for me," Frank called as he rushed into the shop. "Sorry I'm late. My grandma needed me to help her with the laundry. What are we doing?"

Anna explained the raffle, and he looked disappointed. "I don't have any fat quarters," he responded. Frank had only made a couple of table runners and hadn't had an opportunity to collect fat quarters. "Can I buy some?" he asked Anna.

"Here," Delores spoke up. "Take these two and if you win, you can pay me back."

"Thank you," Frank said almost shyly. He had never fit in well with his own age group, but he enjoyed being a part of the quilter's group.

"Here's mine," Caitlyn said, placing one on the pile.

"I'm going to throw in two more fat quarters to make it an even forty," Anna said. She shook the bag that now contained forty scraps of paper with the contributing members' names.

"Who wants to pick the winner?" she asked as she continued to shake the bag. How about you Caitlyn?"

Caitlyn blushed as she always did when she was the center of attention. She reached into the bag and grinned. "Frank," she announced.

"Me?" Frank looked shocked and even a bit worried. "What will I do with all these?" he asked almost rhetorically as he looked at the fabrics. "These are beautiful," he added. "Oh here, Delores," and he picked out the two Delores had given him. She smiled and thanked him.

"Really," he repeated, this time looking from Anna to Sarah. "What will I do with these?"

"How about we all help you make a quilt."

"For my grandmother?"

"Well, it could be, but how about for yourself?" He grinned, apparently liking the idea.

They put their heads together to come up with a simple quilt that they could all work on together. They finally settled on a sashed four-patch, and they began cutting just as soon as they figured out the dimensions. "We'll choose the sashing later," Anna said.

They cut nine six-inch squares from each fat quarter and handed Frank the left-over pieces. "These are for your next project," Delores said. "We'll help you make a scrap quilt." They got Frank started at the machine sewing them together in groups of two and Caitlyn sat at a machine next to him and put his twos into groups of four. Simultaneously, Allison and Sarah did the same thing on the other side of the table. Anna and Delores set up two ironing boards and did the pressing. By 9:00, they had the four-patches completed.

"Do you want to take these home or keep them here," Anna asked.

"I'll leave them here so we can work on them next week," he responded.

While they were cleaning up the work room, Delores asked Sarah about the classes she took at the show.

"I took two classes, one on trapunto and the other on paper piecing," she responded and pulled out the projects she had completed. Delores was familiar with both techniques, but the rest of the group was fascinated and very interested in learning.

"Will you teach us how to do this?" Caitlyn asked as she carefully examined the paper-pieced star.

"Well, Ruth wants me to design a couple of classes for the shop, so maybe I'll practice on you folks." They remained quiet for a moment, as they always did when Ruth's name was mentioned, but then responded favorably, especially Caitlyn who was like a sponge when it came to learning new techniques.

"Sarah, would you be willing to show me how to do trapunto?" Allison asked. "My mother sent me this beautiful cotton panel with an exotic bird in bright shades of blue, red, and yellow. I think they're macaws. Anyway, they're sitting on a limb in a tropical forest, and I'd love to make the bird and the limb stand out and maybe a few of the leaves and flowers when I quilt it. I just don't know where to begin with the trapunto."

"How many people would be interested in learning trapunto?" Anna asked the group, but only two people raised their hands.

"I have at least ten years worth of UFOs in my sewing room. I don't dare start anything new," Kimberly replied.

"I have unfinished projects, too," her sister added, "but don't let us stop you from doing it. I'd be happy to listen."

"I have an idea," Sarah began. "Anna, could we use the classroom one afternoon next week? I'd be happy to go over the instructions with anyone interested, and that'll give me a chance to work out the kinks and be able to offer the class when Ruth gets back. She's had a few customers ask about it, and I know she's interested in offering the class."

"Do you want me to let the customers know about it?" Anna asked.

"Oh no! This is just a practice session for me."

"I don't have anything scheduled in Classroom B this coming week, so just pick a day."

Sarah, Allison, and Caitlyn agreed to get together after the meeting to find a day that was good for them all.

"We forgot to do show-and-tell," Delores announced.

No one had anything except Allison, who pulled out a pile of finished blocks ready to sew into rows.

"What's that pattern called?" Caitlyn asked, and she blushed when the group chuckled at her question.

"Sorry, Caitlyn. We aren't laughing at you. It's just that this block has more names than we could ever list. It's from the early 1800s and one of the first blocks young girls learned to make. I've known it as Hole in the Barn Door, a Love Knot, and a Quail's Nest."

"And back home we called it a Double Monkey Wrench, Hens and Chicks, and Broken Plates," Anna added.

"My grandma has a quilt on her bed like that, and she calls it her Shoo Fly quilt," Frank said.

"I really like it," Caitlyn said, "but it looks hard."

"It's just a nine-patch, Caitlyn. See, three here, three here, and three here," Allison said, pointing to the half square triangles and the blocks between."

"Oh, gosh," Caitlyn replied. "I see it. That *would* be easy."

Allison began gathering up her blocks, and Anna turned to Sarah, "How about you? What have you been working on?"

"I didn't bring anything tonight," Sarah replied, "but I've been working on a Double Wedding Ring quilt."

"Oh my," Delores exclaimed. "You're a brave soul. That's a very complicated pattern."

"Actually," Sarah responded, "I found a simplified technique, and I think it's going to work out just fine. I'll bring it in once I get a little farther along."

"Is this a gift?" Kimberly asked, suspecting Sarah probably had someone in mind.

"Yes, I'm going to save it for the next wedding that comes up. ..."

"The *next* wedding? What do you mean?" Caitlyn asked.

"Well, there's my daughter Martha who just might decide to marry Sophie's Timothy one of these days," Sarah responded. "And then there's Charles' son, David, who is definitely in love with a delightful young woman in Denver named Stephanie. I can hear the faint tinkling of wedding bells in the air—I'm just not sure which direction the sound is coming from." Everyone chuckled knowingly.

"If that's all we have for tonight, let's end the meeting a little early," Anna suggested. "Sarah, do you want to meet with Allison and Caitlyn before you leave?"

The three gathered in the workroom while the others were leaving. "How about Thursday?" Sarah asked.

"I have a doctor's appointment," Allison said. "Could you do Tuesday?"

Looking at her pocket calendar, Sarah said, "Actually, that's even better for me. How about you, Caitlyn?"

"Maybe I shouldn't come. I don't get out of school until 2:30."

"Three o'clock works for me," Sarah said, "You?" she added looking at Allison.

"My husband works from home on Tuesday so he can take care of the kids. Three works fine for me."

"Okay, then. I'll go over my notes and see what I can pull together."

"What should we bring?" Caitlyn asked.

"I'll bring what we need. That's what they did in the class I took, and it worked out just fine. See you girls on Tuesday."

"As they were leaving, Kimberly caught Sarah's eye and raised an eyebrow, symbolically asking if they could talk. Sarah nodded toward the storage room and Kimberly and her sister, Christina, joined her there just as the last person was leaving the shop.

"Has there been any word?" Christina asked as she entered the room.

"Nothing yet, but my husband has gone up to Chicago to help with the investigation."

"That's right," Kimberly responded. "He's a retired policeman, isn't he?"

"Well, he's retired, but he helps out occasionally. He's been there a few days now, and he told me last night that the lead detective is allowing him all the freedom he needs to investigate."

As they were leaving, Kimberly lightened the mood by asking, "Who do you think will spend their honeymoon under that Double Wedding Ring quilt of yours?"

Sarah laughed. "They're all four totally closed-mouthed when it comes to wedding plans, but my guess is that it will be Martha and Timothy. They've been spending lots of time as a family and Martha has lost her fear of potential motherhood. Martha has even taken time off to go on field trips with Penny, which has been a big change. Martha never took time off. Her work was always her life."

"That's a good sign," Christina said walking toward the door.

On her way home, Sarah rolled down the window so she could enjoy the warm spring breeze. Trying to put aside her friend's situation for the time being, she turned her thoughts to Sophie and smiled.

Sophie had skipped the meeting so she could have dinner with her son and his daughter, and Penny was cooking most of the meal. Before her illness, Penny's mother had taught her how to make an authentic Italian lasagna, and Penny was excited about preparing it for her new family. Tonight was just a practice run. Next week, she was going to be preparing it for the entire family at Sophie's party.

"What's this party?" Charles asked when he called later that night.

"I don't know. Sophie said Tim asked her to have it at her house, but they're doing all the work. I know that Martha has been invited. Do you suppose there'll have an announcement?"

"Have you asked your daughter?"

"Martha dismisses the issue every time I bring it up. If there are going to be wedding bells, I guess you and I will learn about it along with everyone else." She sighed with resignation. "That's just the way it is."

"Well, at least you know your son's news," Charles remarked as his voice carried the warm smile she knew was spreading across his face.

Sarah instantly glowed with the joyful smile of a proud grandmother. "Yes, at least I know my son's news."

Jason had called that afternoon to announce that the baby would be a boy. "Little Alaina is going to have a little brother."

* * * * *

The next morning as Sarah was washing the breakfast dishes, the phone rang. She started to let it go to the machine but decided to dry her hands and answer it. She was glad she had when she saw that it was Charles calling.

"Good morning, dear," she answered. "This is a special treat. You usually don't call before the evening," but then she frowned and added, "Is everything okay?"

"I'm on my way home."

"Charles, you've only been there a few days," Sarah responded incredulously. "I thought you'd been cleared to help with the investigation."

"I was, but it's not a police matter any longer. The FBI took it over."

"What?"

"Yep. According to Krakowski, the feds swooped in here early this morning and set up a command center. They've agreed to keep the lieutenant informed, but they refused any involvement by the department and definitely not any help from an outsider like me. I'm heading home as we speak."

"What does this mean, Charles?"

"Not sure, but one thing is certain. This lady was involved in something big."

"Oh, Charles," Sarah responded doubtfully. "I can't believe that. She's a kind, middle-aged woman. She's married, has a grown daughter, and runs a small quilt shop in a peaceful Midwestern town. What could she be involved in that would cause her to be kidnapped, of all things."

"You know what they say about the quiet ones …" Charles joked.

"This isn't funny, Charles. Her family is devastated."

"Sorry, hon. I didn't mean to make light of the situation."

"Oh, Charles," she sighed. "What in the world is going on?"

"No idea, sweetie. I'll be home in a couple of hours. We'll talk more then. Don't mention the FBI to the family just yet, okay?"

"Okay," she replied reluctantly.

As she hung up the house phone, Sarah heard her cell phone ring. She hurried to the kitchen, but as she reached for the phone, she saw Anna's name on the incoming call display. *She'll know I'm holding something back*, she thought. She hesitated a moment, wondering what to do.

She let the call go to voice mail but noticed another message that must have come in while she was talking to Charles. It was Sophie announcing that she and Emma were on their way over.

Moments later, there was a knock at the door. "Come on in, Sophie," Sarah said as she held the screen door open, "and tell me all about your dinner with Tim and Penny."

"What's wrong?" Sophie asked ignoring her friend's words and responding instead to the stressed look on her face.

"It's nothing," Sarah replied, wondering how her friend was able to read her so well. "Come on back to the kitchen. The coffee's on, and I heated up the apple pie we had last night." Sarah started to lead the way, but Sophie continued to stand at the door.

"Sarah, come right back here and answer my question. I know when you're upset, and I want to know what's going on."

Sarah sighed and walked back to the door. "Okay, come back to the kitchen and we'll talk. Charles told me not to tell anyone, but I guess that doesn't mean you. You just have to promise me not to repeat it until it's announced officially. We don't want Ruth's family to hear rumors until we find out exactly what's going on."

"They found her?" Sophie asked, looking frightened. "Was she …?"

"No, no. Nothing like that."

Sarah noticed that her friend was limping and asked her about it. Sophie had a knee replacement the previous year, and Sarah hoped she hadn't developed a problem with it.

"It's the other knee, but I'm scheduled for a pain shot tomorrow. The doc said I'm a long way from needing this one replaced. So, serve the pie, toss some ice cream on top, and tell me what's going on." Emma had bowed to Barney several times and pretended to run away until Barney finally agreed to chase her around their indoor track: through the kitchen, down the hall past the bedrooms, into the living room, across to the dining room, and back to the kitchen only to start all over again until they both were exhausted.

Sarah sliced the pie, poured the coffee, and was scooping ice cream when the dogs finally collapsed on the kitchen floor. "Finally," she said. "Peace and quiet."

"Talk to me," Sophie insisted as she scooped into her pie à la mode.

"Okay, so it's about Ruth. Charles is on his way back from Chicago. …"

"What? I thought he was going to be up there working with the police...."

"That's what I want to explain. They sent him home. It seems the FBI has taken over the investigation, and they're being very secretive. Charles wasn't able to find out anything."

"Oh my. The FBI? What does this mean?" The two friends speculated but were at a loss to figure out why the FBI would get involved. "Isn't there something about kidnapping across state lines or something?" Sophie asked.

"I think so. We'll ask Charles. He should be home soon. So ..." Sarah began, hoping to lighten the mood, "tell me about your dinner with Tim and Penny."

"We had a splendid time," Sophie responded with the enthusiasm of a proud grandmother. "Penny prepared this Italian meal her mother had taught her how to make. She's really something. You know, by the time Timmy got involved, she had been doing all the cooking, caring for the house and her ailing mother—and all that in an isolated cabin without modern conveniences."

"Her mother obviously did an excellent job of raising Penny from what I've seen," Sarah said.

"I agree," Sophie responded as a cloud of sadness crossed her face. "I just wish Betsy had told him about the baby. We could all have been there for them, and I would have known my granddaughter much sooner."

"Betsy did what she thought was best."

"I know."

The two women sat in silence for a while until they heard Charles pull into the garage. Both dogs ran to the garage door barking, whining, jumping, and scratching at the door until Barney accidentally nipped Emma's ear, resulting in the two of them rolling around on the floor in a struggle that appeared to be somewhere between a dog fight and the discovery of a delightful new game. Whatever it was, it stopped the moment Charles opened the door, and they ran to him, both wagging their entire bodies as they each attempted to keep all four feet on the floor—something Charles insisted upon.

"Come have coffee and tell us about Chicago," Sophie said, impatient to hear the whole story.

Charles glanced at Sarah, wondering if he should talk in front of Sophie, and she immediately understood. "I've told Sophie what I know, which isn't much."

"I don't know much more," he responded. "Let me wash up and I'll come sit with you. Is that apple pie I see there?"

"We saved you a sliver."

"Only a sliver?" he asked as he turned the water on in the sink and soaped up his hands with Sarah's sweet-smelling hand soap.

"A heart-healthy sliver," Sarah responded, "and a double scoop of fat-free ice cream."

"Umm," he replied, trying to keep the promise he had made to himself not to complain about his diet. He knew his wife went to great effort to prepare healthy meals for him according to his doctor's instructions, but it really did get hard sometimes. He felt a little guilty about the fast food breakfast he had on the road that morning, but he had decided that he would keep that to himself. *Did I throw that wrapper away?* he wondered as he headed toward the coffee pot.

"What's that guilty look on your face?" Sarah asked.

"Just thinking, dear. Just thinking. Now, what have you two been talking about?"

"Sophie was telling me about her dinner with Tim last night. I think I told you that Penny was trying out a recipe that she planned to use for the party. Penny is doing all the cooking Saturday."

"I keep hearing about this party. What's it all about, Sophie?"

"I don't know any more than you do. Timmy is being very mysterious, but I have my suspicions."

"Wedding bells?"

"Perhaps," Sophie responded, "but right now we want to hear about what's going on up in Chicago."

"Well, as Sarah probably told you, I got thrown out. The feds have moved in and taken over."

"What's going on, Charles?" Sophie frowned.

"I don't know. The FBI won't talk to me at all, and the detective in charge of Ruth's case said they're very secretive with him as well. I did see a couple of guys from the U.S. Marshal's office there, and that made me wonder ..." Charles didn't finish his sentence, and Sarah decided not to press him about it. She knew he probably realized that he was saying more than he should.

"The Marshals?" Sophie exclaimed. "Why would they be there? What's Ruth mixed up in anyway?" Turning to Sarah, she added, "I think we need to get back in the sleuthing business."

That got Charles' attention. "No. Absolutely not," he exclaimed. "You two stay totally out of this one. This is something for the professionals. I don't know what's going on, but I *do* know that none of us should get mixed up in it. Me included, for that matter."

And he fully intended to follow his own advice. *But first,* he thought, *I'll give Jake a call in a few days and see what I can find out … just to satisfy my curiosity,* he assured himself.

Chapter 10

It was the day of the party.

Timothy had set up two six-foot tables in Sophie's backyard and had a fire going in the grill. Penny had two pans of lasagna in the oven and was placing her homemade rolls on a baking sheet. Sophie and Penny had prepared an enormous antipasto platter with rolled salami, slices of pepperoni, black and green olives, mozzarella balls, artichokes, marinated mushrooms, and slivered prosciutto. The wine was chilling, and Tim was placing peppers, onions, and Italian sausage on the grill.

As the guests arrived, Sophie offered them wine and directed them to the backyard, although both Martha and Sarah stayed in the kitchen with Sophie and Penny. Emma was having a playdate with Barney at Sarah's house. Sophie thought the excitement would be too much for her dog, not to mention the temptation of all the food.

"Perfect weather for a party," Martha was saying. She was wearing a pastel sundress with a white sweater over her shoulders. Sarah thought she saw a flicker of sadness cross her face but didn't want to ask, at least not today. She hoped everything was okay between her daughter and Timothy.

When Jason arrived with his wife and daughter, Sarah hurried over to give her son and daughter-in-law a welcoming hug. "How are you feeling?" she asked Jennifer, remembering how much trouble she had when she was pregnant with Alaina.

"So far, I'm feeling great," she responded. Jennifer was a petite woman in her late thirties, a few years younger than Sarah's son. She had been CEO of an electronics firm when she and Jason married, but when Alaina was born, Jennifer had announced that she was resigning to be a full-time mother. Sarah had wondered how she'd adjust to her new life, but she needn't have worried. Jennifer had blossomed in her new role and today her eyes were twinkling as she spoke with excitement about the birth of their son who was expected in the fall. "We're thinking about naming him Jonathan," Jennifer said looking hesitantly into Sarah's eyes for a reaction. "If that's okay with you."

"That would be wonderful," Sarah responded with tears burning at the back of her eyes. "Just wonderful." Jonathan was Sarah's husband, the children's father, who had died when Jason was twenty-one and Martha two years younger. "I'm sure that pleases Jason. He loved his father very much and lost him at a bad time for a boy. He needed his dad to help him with all those decisions a young man must make. I tried...."

"You did an excellent job," Jennifer assured her, resting her hand on Sarah's arm. "Jason is an incredible man."

"So was his father...."

The two women embraced as Charles came into the kitchen carrying Alaina. "You two look very serious. What's going on?"

"Girl talk," Jennifer replied with a smile as she stood on her tiptoes to kiss her daughter's cheek.

"Should I put the rolls in?" Penny asked Sophie. "I took the lasagnas out of the oven."

"I think so. You can let the casseroles rest, and when the rolls are done, you can use the oven to keep everything warm until you're ready to serve."

"Until *I'm* ready to serve?"

"Sure, this is your meal."

Penny blushed and slipped the rolls into the oven.

"Why don't you ask your dad when the sausages will be ready."

"Okay," she responded as she grabbed a bottle of coke and headed for the backyard. "I'll be back in a minute."

"She seems to be enjoying this," Sarah said once Penny was gone.

"I know," Sophie responded. "She told me this morning she'd like to be a chef when she grows up and work in an Italian restaurant. Her mother was Italian, and I guess that has something to do with it. Also, she taught her how to cook when she was very young."

"You know," Sarah began thoughtfully. "Andy's been looking into programs for Caitlyn, and he was talking about that technical school next to the high school. High school students can take classes there as electives in their junior and senior years, and I'm sure they'd have a cooking program. That might be something Timothy could look into next year."

"That's a terrific idea," Sophie replied. "I'll tell Timmy about it. She's only a sophomore now, but it's something to look into."

"Dad's taking the sausages off now and needs something to put them in," Penny announced as she hurried back into the kitchen.

"I'll take something out to him so you can stay here and check on the rolls," Sophie responded as she reached for a shallow baking dish.

Sarah watched the young girl check the rolls and carefully pull the baking sheet out of the oven wearing an oven mitt on each hand. She then turned the oven off and left the door open to cool down. When her father came in red-faced from the grill, she told him to slide the sausages into the oven to keep warm until they were ready to serve. She slipped her two casseroles in as well and set the rolls on the open door. "I'll start rounding up our guests," Sophie announced as she headed for the back door. "Sarah, would you bring that pile of napkins?"

One of the tables had been set for eight, with one place being taken up with Alaina's high chair. The antipasto was sitting in the middle of the table, and everyone was asked to bring their wine glasses and have a seat. Sophie sat at one end of the table, Tim sat at the opposite end with Penny to one side and Martha to the other. Charles and Sarah sat next to Martha while Jason and Jennifer sat on the opposite side with Alaina between them. Once everyone was seated, Tim stood and asked the blessing followed by a touching toast to friends and family.

At that point, Penny stood and picked up the antipasto platter and walked from one guest to the next, offering them the opportunity to serve themselves from the tempting assortment of meats, cheeses, and vegetables. "This is an Italian antipasto," Penny said in a serious and grown up voice. "*Anti* means before and *pasto* means food, so it's served *before food*." Everyone praised the artistry of the dish and commented on each of the ingredients as they sampled them. Penny blushed throughout the entire course and seemed relieved to get away from the table when it was time to serve the main course.

"May I help?" Martha asked as Penny was walking toward the kitchen.

Penny hesitated, then smiled and said, "You could collect the salad plates while I get the main course." Tim refilled the wine glasses and the friends talked and laughed as they waited for Penny to return.

When she and Martha returned, they were carrying the two lasagnas, which they placed at each end of the table. They made one more trip and brought the pan of sausages grilled with peppers and onions, which they sat in the middle of the table along with two baskets of rolls and a bowl of whipped butter. As they were eating and talking, Timothy suddenly started singing in an exaggerated baritone voice, "When the moon hits your eye like a big pizza pie ..."

"Dad!" Penny reprimanded, looking embarrassed.

"It's okay," he responded. "It's Italian. Well, at least it's someone's interpretation of Italian. It was before your time, but it goes with the meal."

"Ah," Sophie interjected. "Dean Martin. I have some of his records. I'll play them for you sometime, Penny."

"Do you still have a record player?" Sarah asked.

"Oh. I forgot about that. Well, there must be some modern way to play his music."

"There are more ways than you could ever imagine!" Charles chuckled as he scooped up another helping of lasagna.

An hour or so later, Timothy tried to stand up but groaned and held his stomach. "What a meal," he said, and Penny smiled proudly. "You did good, young lady."

"That's not all," she said excitedly and ran into the kitchen. She returned with a plate of raspberry tarts, which she passed out as Martha removed their dinner dishes and returned with a tray of cups and the coffee pot.

"This was incredible, Penny," Sarah remarked as she savored the last bite. "Did you make these tarts yourself?"

Penny looked embarrassed for a moment but began telling Sarah what her mother had taught her about making pies and tarts. "It's important that you make the crust just right ... and only use fresh fruit," she added with authority.

Charles caught Sarah's eye and winked.

"More coffee anyone?" Sophie asked. The sun was going down, and there was a cool breeze. "Let's move into the living room."

Sarah started to stack up the dishes, but Timothy reached for her arm. "No, my dear. The men will take care of this. You sit down, and we'll be right in. Come on, guys. We've got work to do."

It was another hour before the men joined the women in the living room. The women were on their second cup of coffee and were playing a hand of rummy when the men finally finished in the kitchen. "We left a couple of things. ..." Timothy said apologetically.

"That's fine son. Get your coffee and come in here. We've patiently waited all day to hear your big news."

"My news? Okay, but I was going to work up to that. Shall I just spill it?"

"Spill it," Sarah and Sophie said in unison as they glanced back and forth between Timothy and Martha.

"Okay. I've been offered a job in Altoona."

Chapter 11

Sarah heard Sophie's car pull into the driveway early the next morning. She opened the door, and Sophie burst into the house and headed for the kitchen. Without a greeting, she started right in. "It's nearly seven-hundred miles from here," Sophie cried. "Seven hundred miles! I've waited thirty-five years for my son to come home from Alaska and fourteen years to get to know my granddaughter."

Sarah knew Sophie really hadn't been waiting for Penny all those years—she didn't even know she had a granddaughter, but Sarah knew what her friend meant. She had no sooner begun to enjoy having her family with her, and here they were being ripped away. Sarah folded up her laptop and returned it to its quilted tote bag. They had been looking at maps and calculating distances. "It's at least an eleven-hour drive," Sophie continued, "and probably another three or four when you count all the stops I'd be making. It would take me *days* to drive there."

"I'm sure they'll visit you here," Sarah replied, but she knew that wasn't the same as having them living right up the street.

"That's not the same!" Sophie muttered. She pushed the plate of cookies aside and said, "Besides, he's retired. Why does he have to have a job anyway? He could ..." but she didn't finish the sentence. Her voice had cracked, and Sarah knew she was holding back her tears.

"Besides," Sophie continued, "he's been up there for thirty-five years."

Sarah replied, "Well, he's still a young man. I can understand why he would want to keep working."

"Well, at least he could find something closer to home."

She searched for something to say to her friend but knew there was nothing she could say that would ease her pain. She knew all she could do was listen and actually that was all Sophie wanted.

"By the way, Sarah," Sophie said, still struggling against the tears that were threatening to flow, "have you heard anything from Martha about all this?"

Sarah hesitated, "Well ..."

"I'm not asking you to break any confidences, but I'm just concerned that she might be having as much trouble as I am. After all ..."

"I guess she wouldn't mind me talking about it, but don't let this get back to Tim. They need to talk directly to one another about it, and I told her the same thing I told you: to talk to him and tell him exactly how she feels."

"How does she feel?" Sophie asked again.

"She's hurt. She's hurt, and she doesn't have any idea how she fits into his life if he can just pick up and move away."

"I can certainly understand that," Sophie remarked.

"She has a good job," Sarah continued, "and surely he doesn't expect her to just quit and follow him."

"Is that what he asked her to do?"

"No," Sarah responded. "According to Martha, he hasn't addressed where this leaves their relationship at all. I told her she should just ask."

"Well," Sophie said as she stood up to leave, "I can sure understand how that poor woman feels. I didn't raise my son to be like this. He doesn't seem to be at all concerned about how he's affecting the people who love him."

"Don't be too hard on him, Sophie."

"Thank you for being there for all of us," Sophie said finally, reaching for Sarah's hand in a rare display of affection. "I could use a fidget quilt about now," she added with a shallow smile."

* * * * *

Anna and Katie were in the storage room sorting through a new shipment of fabrics when they heard the tinkling of the bells on the door, indicating that someone had come into the shop. "I'll be right with you," Anna called as she placed the fabric bolt she was holding back into the container.

"Take your time," the familiar voice responded. "I'll just be looking around."

"Sarah," Anna exclaimed as she came out of the back room. "I thought that was you. What are you doing here so early? Isn't your class at three?" She wanted to ask if Charles had found out anything about the investigation, but she didn't want to bring up a gloomy subject first thing.

"I've had an idea for a wall hanging for Charles' computer room. His birthday is in July, the fourth actually, and I got to thinking about a Log Cabin design in shades of blue with red centers and a white tone on tone. I was looking at these blue batiks, but I'd only need a strip of each one." In fact, Sarah was searching for something to take her mind away from her constant thoughts about Ruth. She had awakened with a start in the middle of the night after having a horrible dream involving her friend. She couldn't seem to stop imagining what might be happening to her.

Neither woman spoke of Ruth.

"I have just the thing," Anna responded enthusiastically. "It just came in," she added as she hurried toward the storage room. "I'll be right back." She didn't return immediately, but when she did, she carried a small roll of fabric which she handed to Sarah. "This is a roll of two-and-a-half-inch strips, all batiks, and all different shades of blue. That's probably more than you'll need for a wall hanging, but it would offer you lots of variety." Sarah noticed that when she returned her eyes were red and swollen.

"This is exactly what I need, and I'll just add the leftovers to my batik collection. I want to make a scrappy batik quilt someday using a braid pattern."

"That would be very striking," Anna said, averting her eyes.

"It's okay to talk about her," Sarah said gently. Anna collapsed in Sarah's arms and sobbed.

* * * * *

Charles had the house to himself, and he took advantage of the time to call his son. "I need help," he said when John answered the phone.

"What can I do for you, Pop?"

"Are you still able to get information from that FBI friend of yours up in Chicago?"

"Seymour Jackson? I'm in touch with him, but he's not in Chicago anymore. He's been reassigned to Texas. He's working on some big drug case. Why do you ask?"

Charles explained the situation and John listened with interest.

"You say the FBI took over the case a few days ago?" John asked.

"That's what the lead detective told me. The department's been totally cut out of the loop, and I can't find out a thing. Do you think your friend might be able to find out what's going on?"

"I'm not sure they'll be willing to share details about their investigation...." John began.

"No, I'm just trying to find out why the FBI would be involved at all. This is a middle-aged woman who runs a small quilt shop and leads a quiet life. We just want to know why the FBI and the Marshals would be involved in investigating her disappearance...."

"Wait a minute!" John interrupted. "You say the Marshals? The U.S. Marshals Service?"

"Well, Jake, he's the detective up there, told me that the Marshals arrived along with the FBI agents. What do you suppose that means?"

"Whew. I don't know, Dad, but this lady is sure not who you think she is. The Marshals are in charge of fugitive operations and work out of the federal court system. This lady must be big time."

"No, John! I can't believe that. I know this woman. She's Amish, for Christ's sake!"

"Not a bad cover," John chuckled.

Charles sighed. "There something we're missing here."

"Well, the only other thing I can think of is that the Marshals also operate the Federal Witness Protection Program. Could she have been in the program and gotten picked up by the bad guys?"

Charles was speechless. "That hardly fits with what I know about her."

"You may not know this lady at all, Pop."

"I just don't know. Let me think about this. In the meantime, would you talk to this Seymour and see what you can find out?"

"I'll ask, but I can't guarantee anything. If this goes as deep as it sounds like it might, he's not going to be able to talk."

"I understand."

After a short silence, John changed the subject saying, "We sure enjoyed having you and Sarah here last month. I hope we can do that again."

"We plan to make it an annual event if that's okay with you folks."

"We'd love it.

After they hung up, Charles sat rubbing his forehead and trying to make sense of what he had just learned. He wondered how much he should share with Sarah and decided he would, at least for now, keep this disturbing information to himself.

Chapter 12

"Good afternoon, class," Sarah began very formally, and her two students laughed.

Sarah knew that Allison was familiar with the concept of trapunto, but since she was practicing for an actual class, and since she wasn't sure how much Caitlyn might know about it, she started by defining trapunto and passing around the sample she had made in her own class. "My instructor called it 'stuffed quilting.' "

It became immediately obvious that Caitlyn had no idea what she had signed up for once she saw the sample. She gasped with amazement and exclaimed, "I had no idea you could do this." Sarah saw her turn it over and examine the small hand stitches on the back and smile.

She gets it already, Sarah thought. Caitlyn, she knew, would be a fantastic quilter one day.

Sarah then passed out the fabric packets she had prepared. She had used a twelve-inch piece of fabric that featured a large rose with a stem and two leaves. The rose was red on a white background with green leaves and stems. To save time, Sarah had placed a piece of muslin behind the fabric square and had outline stitched around the rose, the stem, and the leaves with her machine. She went over the process so her students would know how to do this part themselves in the future.

She then gave each of her students a small bag of polyester filling and stilettos she had borrowed from Anna. Using the fabric packet she had made for herself, she illustrated how to cut a small slit in the middle of the rose on the muslin side. "Be very careful not to cut your rose."

Allison and Caitlyn pinched their muslin and carefully snipped.

"Now, you just want to start stuffing the polyester filling inside until it's stuffed as tight as you want it. Just look at the front and stop when you're happy with the way it looks," she added.

"Now what?" Allison asked once she was finished stuffing.

"Just whipstitch to close the slit. She handed Allison a needle and thread and another set to Caitlyn, who wasn't quite ready.

"How about the stem?" Allison asked, seeing that Sarah had also stitched the length of the stem on both sides.

"Let's do the leaf next," Sarah said, "and go ahead and do that one by yourself." Once they had finished, Sarah talked about several techniques for stuffing the stems, and then they practiced on the stem that Sarah had outline-stitched.

"This isn't as easy as the rose," Caitlyn commented.

"It will be easier with practice, or at least so my instructor said," Sarah assured her with a chuckle. "Just try several techniques at home until you're comfortable."

The sun was shining into the room and across Caitlyn's face. Her hair glistened, and she had a gentle smile. She was wearing a pale pink blouse and new jeans. She looked happy.

Sarah couldn't help but compare the picture with the same young girl two years ago, living alone on the street, sleeping in crowded shelters and alleys, learning from the homeless how to survive. *Thank you, God*, she said under her breath, and she turned her back to the class to hide the emotion she was feeling.

"This is such fun," Caitlyn exclaimed. "I can't wait to try it out on the pillow I'm making for Papa's chair."

Sarah chuckled when Caitlyn's comment yanked her back to the present. She then pulled several types of stuffing from her tote bag and talked about the advantages of each. She also showed them how they can draw their pattern on a solid piece of fabric, back it, machine or hand stitch the lines, and stuff it to form the a pattern. "That makes a stunning quilt. I saw one at the show with an allover pattern of feathers. The texture and depth were breathtaking."

"You can learn more online by simply doing a search on trapunto tutorials," she added. "When I do the actual class, people will leave with a finished wall hanging, but I know you two don't want to spend that much time here today."

"Sarah, before we go," Allison said, reaching into her tote bag, "I brought my panel. Can you help me decide what parts to stuff?" She pulled it out and the three spent time deciding what parts would befit from trapunto. "I want the bird to stand out the most," she said.

"You could actually put extra stuffing in the birds head and peak," Sarah suggested, "and make those parts stand out even more than the body."

"And I think one of those flowers over here would look good stuffed and, of course, the limb," Caitlyn suggested. "The fabric I'm using for Papa's pillow is something like this, only it has a peacock. He loves peacocks. I'm glad I haven't sewn it together yet because I want to use trapunto on parts of it, maybe the feathers."

"I hope you'll bring it to our meeting when you finish," Allison commented.

Allison wasn't much older than Caitlyn, but was married and had children. Sarah knew her mother and knew that Allison had gone from her parent's home to her marriage. The two girls were worlds apart and yet they sat, heads together, planning their projects and giggling.

Looking at her panel, Allison said, "This is going to be phenomenal. I can hardly wait for my mother to see it. I'm sure this isn't what she had in mind when she said I could 'finish it off.'"

Sarah saw a moment of sadness cross Caitlyn's face at the word *mother*.

* * * * *

The next afternoon, there was a light tapping on the front door that Sarah could hardly hear. She pulled the curtain aside and saw Caitlyn looking worried. Sarah opened the door and greeted her enthusiastically, but the girl's first response was an apology.

"I'm so sorry to come by without calling, Aunt Sarah." Sarah was in no way related to the young girl, but both Caitlyn and Penny had started calling her Aunt. Sarah liked it. Being from a small family, she didn't have nieces and nephews. Her only sister had died in her early twenties not long after her marriage. Caitlyn and Penny, for that matter, didn't have but a few relatives and Sarah understood their need for family.

"You never have to call, my dear. I love opening the door and finding you there," she responded as she hugged the child fondly. At that moment, Barney came galloping into the room and right out the front door.

"Oh, Barney," Caitlyn cried. Turning to Sarah, she said, "I'll get him," but it wasn't necessary. He was so happy to see Caitlyn that he was immediately by her side, smiling and panting.

"Come on in, Caitlyn, and have refreshments. I was just getting ready to have my afternoon snack."

"You have a snack in the afternoon?" Caitlyn said somewhat surprised. She always had a snack when she got home from school, but it never occurred to her that an adult might do that as well.

Sarah put two glasses of milk on the kitchen table along with a platter of cookies, but they remained untouched as Caitlyn sat quietly rubbing Barney's head. Sarah sensed that Caitlyn had something on her mind. "Was there something you wanted to talk about, Caitlyn?"

"Oh, Aunt Sarah, I don't know if I should be telling you this, but I just don't know what to do. I wanted to talk to you about it after our class yesterday, but it didn't seem like the right time."

"What is it, Caitlyn?" Sarah asked, becoming concerned. She rarely saw the girl without a smile on her face.

"It's just that Penny is so upset about moving to Altoona. She doesn't want to go."

"Well honey, sometimes parents have to move with their jobs. The kids never want to do it. It means leaving their school and their friends, but Penny is a smart young lady, and I know she'll adjust well. Has she told her father how she feels?"

"She doesn't want to tell him. She wants to ask her grandmother if she can go live with her."

Sarah didn't know how to respond. It made her very sad to think that Penny was faced with losses again. She'd gone through many changes in the past year, and she had made many adjustments. It seemed like she had finally found her place in her new life. From the day Timothy made his announcement about moving, Sarah had wondered how it would affect Penny.

"This is really between Timothy and his daughter, Caitlyn," Sarah began. "I don't know what we can do. They need to be talking to each other so that her father knows how she feels and can help her adjust to the idea of moving. In fact, Sophie also needs to know what Penny has in mind."

"Would you talk to Sophie?"

"Me?"

"She'd listen to you. Someone has to help Penny."

Sarah thought about it for a minute and reluctantly agreed to talk to Sophie. "But please talk to Penny and make sure it's okay with her for me to get involved."

"It is," Caitlyn responded, looking relieved.

"It is? How do you know that?"

"She's the one that suggested it."

Sarah laughed, remembering how her own children could always maneuver her into doing exactly what they wanted. "Okay, I'll talk to Sophie, but you let Penny know that what I'm going to suggest is that they all three sit down together and talk about this."

Caitlyn nodded her agreement and reached for a cookie and took a big bite out of it. She immediately made a face and took a large gulp of milk to wash it down. "Oh, sorry," Sarah said, removing the dish and replacing it with chocolate chip cookies. "Those are Charles' special cookies."

"Charles likes those?" she asked, looking skeptical.

"Not really, but that's all he gets. His doctor wants him on a low-fat diet, and I found that recipe online the other day. Not so good, huh?"

"I guess they're okay," Caitlyn responded still holding what was left of the original cookie. Glancing up to see that Sarah wasn't looking, she quickly offered it to Barney who was not so particular.

"Would you like to see the pictures from our trip to Denver?" Sarah asked.

"Oh, yes. What did you do there?"

"Well, we spent a couple of days in the Rocky Mountain National Park driving through the mountains. We walked around in an old mining town from the 1800s, and it looked just like they look in those western movies. Oh, and I saw my first moose!"

"A moose?"

"Actually, a whole herd grazing in the valley." As she talked, Sarah pulled out the appropriate pictures which Caitlyn studied in great detail. "And of course, we saw eagles and elk. Once we got into the higher peaks, the sign said we were at 12,000 feet, and the scenery was breathtaking. Here's a picture of the landscape. See how the mountains in the distance look purple?"

"Oh, that's beautiful! But wasn't it cold?"

"Sure, but it was April, and you could tell spring was coming, at least in the valleys. Wildflowers were beginning to bloom at the lower elevations, and there was snow when we traveled higher. It was a spectacular trip that I'll never forget." She laid out another three or four pictures.

"Didn't his sons go with you to the park? I don't see any pictures of them."

"No, they were working. It was just the two of us. We spent the night at a mountain lodge just outside the park and drove on back to Denver the next day."

"What else did you do while you were there?"

"Well, let's see." Sarah opened the second package of pictures that Charles had picked up the previous day. "We all signed up for a walking tour of Denver, but that turned out to be a mistake. It was the coldest day we had there, and the wind was howling. We went to the top of the state capitol building for a spectacular 360-degree view of the city. Here are several pictures Charles took up there. We abandoned the tour after that and spent the next few hours in a cozy restaurant just getting to know one another. David is the principal of an inner city school, and he had some incredible tales to tell."

"I guess those schools can be pretty rough. We're lucky here."

Sarah scattered the rest of the pictures out, mostly of his sons and John's family, and Caitlyn asked about each one. "How old is John's son?"

"Jimmy's nine and smart as a whip. I think he'll be a lawyer like his father. You should see that boy argue until he gets his way," she added with a loving smile.

"What's this?" Caitlyn asked, holding up a picture of two men who appeared to be racing through the snow in a vehicle of some kind. Sarah laughed as she reached for the picture. "That's John and Charles on snowmobiles. I guess David took that picture. I hadn't seen it."

"You had snow while you were there?"

"Only in the mountains. The men drove up there, but I stayed home and went shopping with John's wife. They came home wet and nearly frozen—I was glad I didn't go."

"I guess I should be getting home," Caitlyn said as she stood up and brushed cookie crumbs into her hand. Barney stood and followed her to the trash can. "Do you think Barney would like a quick walk around the block?"

"He'd love it," Sarah responded as she clicked the leash onto his collar and gave the young girl a quick hug.

"Thank you, Aunt Sarah," she said with a look of relief. "Penny will be so glad you're going to help her."

As Sarah closed the door behind them, she chuckled to herself as two old-time entertainers came to mind. Scolding herself for agreeing to get involved in the Ward's problems, she quoted them aloud, "Well, here's another fine mess you've gotten me into."

Chapter 13

"I think you should stay out of it," Charles was saying as he dipped into his chicken stew.

"They're my friends, Charles, and I've been asked to help."

"You haven't been asked by *them*," he pointed out but noticed that she was now frowning. He decided to let it drop. If she was just going to get them talking to each other, he supposed that didn't count as interfering. *It might even be helpful*, he told himself.

"So I talked to your boyfriend, Jake, today."

Sarah started to object to being teased about Jake again but decided to let it go. This would, at least, get them off the subject of Penny and Tim. "Oh? What did he have to say?"

"Not much. The FBI is playing this close to the vest. He was able to speak with one of the Marshals, though. They recognized each other in a pub up the street from the station and had a beer together. The guy told Jake that they had a lead."

Sarah looked up abruptly. "Really? What?"

"Jake said that the Marshal couldn't give him any details, but that it was encouraging."

"Hmm." Sarah looked back down at her bowl and sighed. "That's not much."

"It's better than nothing.

"True."

They had eaten early, and Sarah was feeling at loose ends after she cleaned up the kitchen. Charles said he was going to walk up to the gym at the community center and work out and asked if she'd like to go with him.

"I don't think so, Charles, but I'm glad you're getting back into the routine."

Once she heard the front door close, Sarah hurried to her sewing room and pulled out the pattern she was planning to use to make his birthday wall hanging. Wanting to try a new pattern, she had changed her mind about doing a Log Cabin and had returned to Stitches to purchase a second package of two-and-a-half-inch strips, this time in shades of cranberry batik to use with the blues she had purchased earlier in the week. Her new pattern was more colorful and was made primarily with half-square triangles. She knew Charles would be gone for at least two hours, and she'd have time to cut it out.

She had no sooner spread the fabrics out on her cutting board when she heard the front door open and Charles anxiously calling her. She quickly bundled up the project and stuck it in her cabinet. "Charles?" she said as she hurried into the living room, wondering why he had returned so quickly.

"It's Sophie," he said breathlessly. "Do you have Tim's cell phone number?"

"What is it Charles?!" she cried. "What's wrong with Sophie?"

"I don't know. I just saw an ambulance pulling away from her house, and Tim was following behind it. I tried to get his attention, but he didn't see me."

"Here's the number," Sarah said frantically handing him her phone book. "I'll use my cell and call Tim's house. Penny might be there alone."

"When Penny answered the phone, she sounded fine. Sarah assumed she didn't know what was happening. "Is your dad home?" Sarah asked, knowing the answer but wanted to find out what Penny knew.

"He went over to Grandma's house to fix her garbage disposal. Do you want me to call him?"

"No, that's fine. I'll talk to him later." Not wanting to upset the young girl, Sarah hung up and turned to Charles, who was now speaking to Timothy.

"What is it, Charles? What's wrong with Sophie?"

"She had a fall," he said motioning for her to wait until he finished.

"Tell him we'll get Penny and bring her over here."

Charles relayed the message and later told Sarah that Timothy sounded relieved. He hadn't called his daughter to tell her what had happened because he was afraid it would frighten her, and she was there alone.

"Ask him if we should go to the hospital?"

"Do you want us to bring Penny and come to the hospital?" Charles asked. He listened to Timothy's answer and shook his head letting Sarah know he didn't want them to come.

As soon as he hung up, Charles pulled Sarah into his arms and reassured her that Sophie would be okay. "Tim found her on the kitchen floor when he got there. She said she slipped on the kitchen floor and couldn't get to the phone. He said Emma was curled up against her and growled at him protectively when he approached her. He tried to help her up, but she was in too much pain, so he called the rescue squad."

"Maybe we should go by there and pick up Emma too."

"You have a key?" Charles asked.

"It's in the flower box," she responded, and Charles frowned. Before he had a chance to complain about Sophie's lack of security, she changed the subject. "I'll call Penny and tell her we're on our way. We can explain about Sophie when we get there."

Even though Sarah didn't know any details yet, she was able to downplay the situation and Penny seemed content with the idea of picking up Emma and perhaps even missing school the next day.

"Can I bring Blossom?" she asked.

"You certainly may," Sarah assured her, wondering how they would survive having three dogs in the house.

"If they keep your grandmother overnight, we'll go see her in the morning," Sarah had assured Penny later that night as she tucked her into bed in the guest room with Blossom snuggled up against her and Emma protectively curled up on the rug next to the bed. Barney watched from the doorway but seemed to understand that it wasn't playtime.

As it turned out, Sophie had fractured her ankle, this time requiring surgery to insert a pin for stability. The same bone had been fractured a couple of years before, and Doctor Dean felt it was unlikely to heal properly this time without the pin. He wanted to keep her for a couple of days, and said she would need to use crutches for three or four weeks while it was healing.

Timothy had stopped by the house later that night to see Penny and let Sarah and Charles know what the doctor had said. "Mom took the news well, and she's already entertaining the nurses with her crazy anecdotes." Timothy, on the other hand, appeared very troubled. "She's going to be okay this time, but …"

Sarah knew he was getting worried about moving away, and she hoped that this would remind him why he had chosen to live close to his mother in the first place. He looked in on Penny and agreed to leave her there since she was sleeping peacefully.

"We will all come to the hospital in the morning," Sarah assured him as he was leaving.

"Thank you, Sarah. You're a good friend to Mom."

"She's a good friend to me," Sarah responded.

Chapter 14

"Tim's on the phone, Charles. He wants to come get Blossom. Will you be here? I'm going out." They had all visited Sophie that morning, and Penny had gone home with her father.

"Tell him I'm going to walk all three dogs soon," Charles replied. "We'll walk on over to his house."

After Sarah had hung up, Charles asked, "Where are you going?"

"Sophie wants her appliqué project. I'm going to run by her house to pick it up, then head on over to the hospital for a couple of hours. I have some hand sewing to do, so I'll take it with me, and we can stitch together."

"Don't you want me to go with you?"

"No, you stay home and spend time with the dogs. I think Emma's beginning to get worried." *Also, I need some private time with Sophie*, she thought but didn't say.

"A romp in the park will take care of that. Could you and I drive over to Sophie's before you leave so I can get more food for Emma?"

"Sure. Let's go now."

All three dogs tried to push their way out the door when Charles and Sarah were leaving. "Don't worry, guys. We'll be right back." While they were at Sophie's, Sarah washed the few pans that were in the sink and started the dishwasher. "What do you suppose caused her to fall?" Sarah asked looking around the kitchen.

"My guess is that she was standing on this stool and fell." Charles picked up a small wooden step stool which was turned on its side.

"She told me she didn't know how she fell, but she told Tim she slipped on the kitchen floor, so I was already getting suspicious," Sarah responded, shaking her head. "I guess she didn't want to admit that she was climbing on that stool again."

"She's fallen off of it before?"

"Twice that I know of."

"I think I'll hide it in the garage and stop by the hardware store tomorrow for one of those step stools with a tall handle."

"She shouldn't be climbing up several steps. That just gives her farther to fall," Sarah responded.

"No, the one I'm thinking of just has one step only about nine inches off the floor and a tall handle that will come practically to Sophie's chest."

"That would solve the problem, Charles," she responded, smiling at her thoughtful husband. "Thank you for that."

All three dogs met them at the door with unbridled enthusiasm despite their short absence, but once Emma felt they had been adequately welcomed, she looked past them, and her ears drooped with disappointment. "Your mommy will be back soon, sweetie," Sarah said rubbing the dog's head and ears. Emma's tail began to wag again, and Sarah hoped she understood.

"I'm going to Tim's house by way of the dog park," Charles announced, reaching for the hook which now held all three leashes. Timothy and Penny lived on the other side of the park. "If Penny calls, tell her I'll be there in about an hour."

"I won't be here," Sarah called over her shoulder as she headed for her sewing room to get her project and sewing box. "I'm leaving right now." She was eager to have some private time with Sophie so they could talk about Penny and the move to Altoona. Sarah hoped her friend wouldn't be too medicated to have a serious conversation.

She needn't have worried. She heard Sophie's voice as she got off the elevator and spotted her coming down the hall awkwardly, getting the feel of her crutches. "I've been visiting my neighbors," she announced as she approached Sarah.

"Good for you," Sarah laughed. "Are you ready for some serious stitching?"

"You brought my appliqué?" Sophie cried excitedly.

Once they were back in Sophie's room, Sarah pulled two guest chairs up to Sophie's bed and the two friends sat down. They used the bed to spread out their material and settled down to sew. Sophie examined Sarah's quilt and asked a few questions about technique. She then asked the question that was really on her mind. "Now tell me honestly," Sophie began, "Is this for Martha and Timmy? Do you know something I don't know?"

"Absolutely not, Sophie. It may well end up going to them, but I don't know any more than you do. In fact,

I seriously wonder what this move to Altoona will mean to their relationship."

"I know," Sophie responded, suddenly looking solemn. "And I don't know what it will do to Penny either."

Sarah was relieved to see that getting around to talking about Penny wasn't going to be difficult at all. Taking advantage of the opening, Sarah said, "Actually, I wanted to talk with you about that. Penny is planning to ask if she can stay here with you. ..."

"That's out of the question," Sophie responded, shaking her head and frowning. "She belongs with her father. They're still getting to know each other. No, that's out of the question. Has she talked to Tim about this?"

Sarah could see her friend was becoming agitated, and she laid her hand on Sophie's arm. "I'm sorry, Sophie. I didn't mean to upset you, but ..."

"It's not you, Sarah. I'm already upset. I can't understand why my son would pick a time like this to move away. Here he is with a child who is beginning to get settled in a new life, and didn't he tell us all how happy he was to finally be living near me? Do you think it's something I've done? Have I ...?"

"Stop, Sophie. You know this has nothing to do with you. I don't know what he has in mind, but moving away right now would be a terrible mistake. Of course, it's his mistake to make. It's none of my business, but I feel very bad for Penny."

"I agree. Do you think there's anything we can do?"

"I think it would be good for the three of you to sit down and talk, and for everyone to be open and honest about their feelings."

"With Penny?" Sophie asked skeptically. "She's so young."

"Absolutely with Penny. She has very strong feelings about this, and they need to be expressed. And so do you. And, for that matter, so does Timothy."

The two friends sewed in silence for a while, each lost in thought. Suddenly Sophie stopped sewing and looked Sarah in the eye. "You're right, and we'll do it Sunday."

"Sunday?" Sarah looked surprised. *That was easier than I expected*, she told herself.

"I'm going home Sunday morning, and we're sitting down in the afternoon. This needs to be hashed out, and Penny needs to be told that she's an equal in this discussion. I want her to be as honest as I intend to be."

"Then tell her that," Sarah responded.

"I will," Sophie said with determination. "He might still move away, but he'll go knowing just how Penny and I feel."

"And you'll know how he feels—why he feels the need to take a job so far away."

"Hmm. Do I really want to hear that one?"

"Yes, you do. That's part of being in an honest relationship. It has to go both ways."

"How did you get so smart?" Sophie teased her friend.

"Probably from hanging out with you," she responded with a wink.

* * * * *

When Timothy opened the door, the three dogs rushed in and headed straight for Penny. She fell to the floor and hugged them all simultaneously while they wiggled, wagged, licked, and barked their excitement. She reached for a toy and tossed it across the room. Both the bigger dogs streaked after it, but Blossom ignored them and stretched her tiny length up and began smothering Penny with kisses. Penny looked like she was going to weep with joy.

"What a pair those two are," Tim remarked adding, "How about a beer?"

They took their drinks into the living room where Timothy had been watching a baseball game. "What's the score," Charles asked, not being much of a fan, but it was always a good icebreaker.

The two men talked about the game for a few minutes, then fell silent. Penny had taken all the dogs into her room along with a bag of treats.

Finally Charles, looking somewhat apologetic, said, "Tell me if I'm intruding, Tim, but I just have to ask you something."

"Go ahead, Charles. I don't have any secrets—well, not many anyway," he added with a nervous chuckle when he thought about Martha and hoped Charles wasn't going to ask about their future plans. He wasn't ready to talk about that, and for that matter, neither was Martha.

"Why do you want to move away?"

Tim looked at Charles thoughtfully for a moment before answering. He then took a deep breath and said, "It's not that I want to move away, Charles. It's hard to explain, but I've worked since I was seventeen years old, and here I am in my fifties and suddenly not working. I don't know how to do this."

"So get a job, but Altoona?"

"There aren't a lot of jobs around for someone trained on the Alaska pipeline," Timothy responded somewhat cynically. "This outfit in Altoona made the only offer I've had."

"What would you be doing?"

"It's a mining outfit. I'd be overseeing safety, and, believe me, I don't feel all that comfortable about it. Pipeline safety and mining safety don't have much in common. I don't know Charles. Penny has hardly talked to me since I announced it, and now with Mom falling and all. I just don't know what to do."

Hesitating a moment, Charles asked, "Sorry if this is too personal, but does your retirement from Alaska give you enough to get by?"

"Sure, enough to get by and then some. It's not the money. It's just … I don't know, Charles, I guess I just don't know what to do with myself if I'm not working. Actually, it's even more than that. I feel worthless when I'm not working. You know I love Sarah's daughter, and I'd love to spend the rest of my life with her, but how can I expect a professional woman to marry an unemployed bum."

"We retired guys aren't bums, my friend. There's plenty to do. How about doing something entirely different? For example," Charles continued, "I've always thought I'd enjoy working in a hardware store."

"They only hire the kids these days, so they don't have to pay much," Timothy responded. "I looked into that."

"So, undercut the kids. You said you don't care about the money, you just want something to do. You'd be a valuable guy to them. These kids can't answer questions."

"I don't know about retail. …" Timothy replied hesitantly.

"Also, there's an abundance of volunteer jobs at the hospital, local nursing homes, even transportation for those old folks right here in the village. Or how about teaching at the community center?"

"Teaching? Teaching what?" Tim was beginning to look interested.

"What are you interested in? Computers? Carpentry?"

"It's something to think about, Charles," Tim responded thoughtfully. "How about another beer?"

"Nah, I should get on home, but come on by if you want to talk more about this. By the way, have you officially accepted the Altoona job?"

"Not officially, but I led this guy to expect me up there in a couple of weeks."

"Well, hold off and take your time. Make sure this is what's best for you and Penny."

"Thanks, pal. You've given me something to think about. Hey, the games over. Who won?"

"I don't even know who was playing," Charles responded with a chuckle. "I've never been much for sports."

"I like baseball," Timothy said. "I coached a company team up north."

"Well, there you go."

"What do you mean?"

"Little league? Or maybe get these old men in the village out on the field. They'd love it." He saw a glimmer of interest cross Timothy's face.

As he was snapping Barney's leash onto his collar, he noticed that Penny was in the hallway grinning ear to ear. *She heard everything we said*, he realized regretfully. He hated giving her hope if none was there.

Later that evening as they were having dinner, Charles told Sarah about his conversation with Tim. Sarah laid down her fork and looked her husband in the eye. "And you told *me* to stay out of it. ..."

They both laughed when he responded with, "Well, I guess we're just a couple of old busybodies."

Chapter 15

"She's been gone now for thirteen days," Anna was saying when Sarah arrived at Stitches the next evening for their second Friday night club meeting without Ruth. Anna was in the back room speaking to someone Sarah didn't recognize. "Oh, Sarah," Anna said when she saw her arrive. "Come in and meet Aunt Joy."

"Aunt Joy?" Sarah hadn't heard mention of an aunt before. She turned the corner and saw an elderly woman dressed in a long sleeve blue cotton dress covered with a black apron. She wore a white cap that Ruth had told her was called a prayer cap. She appeared ageless, but if Sarah had to guess, she would say the woman was probably in her seventies. Sarah was surprised to see her, knowing that both Ruth and Anna had been shunned by their community for marrying outside the Amish community. "I'm very happy to meet you," Sarah responded.

"You look surprised to see my aunt," Anna said, "and believe me, I nearly fainted when she arrived this afternoon."

"I was worried about my nieces," Joy explained in broken English. "We heard about Ruth and I had to come. The bishop gave me permission to come for one day," she added turning to Anna.

"How did you get here," Sarah asked, remembering that the Amish didn't own cars.

"An English family up the road drove us to the bus station, and we hired a taxi when we got to Middletown."

"We?" Anna asked, looking startled.

"Jacob is with me."

"Jacob," Anna cried. She hadn't seen her brother for over fifteen years. "Where is he?"

"He didn't come to the shop," Joy responded. "He's waiting at the bus station."

Anna's face fell with disappointment. "He didn't approve, did he?" she said sadly.

"No, but he was willing to come with me. Your brother took good care of us after your folks died. Jacob let us move into the *grossdaadi haus* on the farm."

"I'm glad, Aunt Joy. I often think about you and uncle...." but as she said it, she saw a flicker of pain cross the elderly woman's face and she knew her husband was gone. Anna patted the hand of her mother's stoic sister. "I'm sorry."

Turning to Sarah, she said, "I've caught Aunt Joy up on what I know about Ruth's disappearance. I told her you were coming, and that you might have more information. Has Charles spoken with anyone in Chicago?"

"He has, but since the FBI took over there hasn't been any new information—at least none we're able to know." The three women were still in the back room when the front door opened, and four or five club members entered chatting excitedly.

"What's going on?" Anna called out to them as she and Sarah joined them.

"Myrtle has an idea she wants to tell us about."

"It sounds like she already has," Sarah said laughing. "Let us in on it."

"Wait," Anna interrupted. "First let me introduce my Aunt Joy. She came down to find out about Ruth, but she's heading home and can't stay for our meeting." At that moment, the front door opened again, and Nathan arrived to drive Anna's aunt back to the bus station.

Taking him aside, Anna whispered, "Jacob is waiting at the station. If you can, tell him I love him."

"I will," he assured her with a sad smile. He knew how much she missed the young man who was only a toddler when she left.

Everyone said goodbye and wished Anna's aunt a safe journey. "I wish Katie could have met her," Anna said to Sarah once the car pulled away from the curb. "Nathan convinced her to go back to Paducah. There's nothing she could do here but worry, and her father thought that her job at the museum would give her something else to think about."

Once everyone was seated at the worktable, Anna said, "Tell us about your idea, Myrtle."

Myrtle got up and walked to the head of the table, and Sarah couldn't hold back her surprise. "Myrtle," she cried. "Look how good you're getting around. You could barely walk last year when you were in my class." She wondered why she hadn't noticed before, but the only time she'd seen Myrtle was the night of the special meeting, and her mind had never left Ruth that night.

"I know," the octogenarian responded proudly. "You told me that I should do what the doctor said and have that hip replacement, and you were right. I can get around now, and I can even play with my great-grandchildren," she added with a proud smile.

"So tell us about your idea," Sarah said.

"Well, it's not really *my* idea, but when I was in the nursing home after my surgery, they put me in a room with this woman who had old-timers' disease." Sarah smiled at the term which she assumed was a distortion of the word Alzheimer's. She'd heard it used before, particularly with older people. "So, anyway," Myrtle continued, "this lady had a visitor who brought her this little quilt she called a fidget quilt. Before Agnes had that little quilt, she'd moan and carry on all the time, but after she got it she'd sit up and, well ..." Myrtle paused for a moment and then continued, "I guess you'd say she *fidgeted* with it. It had buttons and zippers and snaps that she could worry with. There was this fringe around the edges. She let me hold it once, and I realized it had different kinds of touchy fabrics like fleece, fake fur, and even shiny satin. I just thought it might be something we could do for those poor folks over in Twilight Manor."

Sarah smiled as she listened to Myrtle and saw the excitement among the members. She started to say something about the quilt Ruth had bought at the show, but she decided to wait and not interrupt Myrtle, who was clearly enjoying the group's attention.

"How big was this quilt?" Christina asked.

"Oh, I'd say it was only about twenty-four inches square," she responded as she returned to her seat and reached into her purse. "I had my granddaughter take this picture." She handed it to Christina who studied it and passed it on to the others.

Everyone was fascinated with the picture and thought it would be a great project for the club.

"I read about something like this in my nursing magazine," Allison commented as she looked at the picture. "They called them "sensory stimulation quilts" and they can have a calming, soothing effect. They're using them therapeutically for people with dementia and stroke patients."

"I didn't know you were a nurse," Anna commented.

"Actually, I'm not practicing right now. I had just started working when I got pregnant with Nicky, and I decided to stay home with him for a year or two. I just try to keep up by reading the journals."

Once Myrtle was clearly finished with her presentation and had returned to her seat, Sarah reached into her tote bag saying, "This is quite a coincidence." She pulled out the fidget quilt that Ruth had purchased at the show, and everyone gasped in surprise.

"Where did you get this?" Anna asked. Everyone stood up to see it more closely.

"This is Ruth's," Sarah responded.

"What ...?"

"Let me explain." Sarah told them about the last day in Chicago when they were all still together. "Ruth found a vendor who was selling these and she knew right away that we would all love it. She was going to ask if we could take this on as a project for the dementia wing of the nursing home."

"My answer is absolutely yes."

"Mine too."

"Let's see how many we can get made before Ruth comes home," Delores said. Sarah smiled to herself realizing that Delores had adopted her tactic of simply assuming Ruth would be returning.

"I think it's a fantastic idea," Anna responded. "We can use our scraps of interesting fabrics and take a field trip into town to the craft shop to get some other types of fabric—fabrics with texture like chenille, velvet, and even shiny fabrics."

"… and fringe," Caitlyn said. "And we should use very colorful fabrics and familiar designs like cats and dogs, cars, barnyard animals, …"

"Yes, and I like the idea of having things like zippers, snaps, and buttons that work. Maybe a pocket if we can think of something to attach that can be put into it."

"How about attaching a small furry animal, something like a dog toy that squeaks?"

"My grandmother has these yarn balls that I think would feel good to touch," Frank added, eager to contribute.

The ideas continued to fly as their excitement grew. "This will be great fun," Sarah said. It made her happy to see her friends smiling and full of enthusiasm for the first time since she returned from Chicago.

"Thank you, Myrtle, for sharing this with us."

The group discussed the idea of fidget quilts and decided to start making them at the very next meeting. "Bring in everything you have around the house that you think would be good," Anna said, "and I'll provide the fabric."

Sarah noticed that Kimberly and Christina were talking about the various items they could bring, and Myrtle was saying that her grandchildren had things they'd probably contribute. Sarah couldn't think of anything she might have, but decided to stop at the craft shop and pick up some beads and fringe. She also thought she could get some pieces of yarn from Sophie.

Before they left for home, several women asked about Sophie. "She'll be coming home on Sunday," she assured them. Sarah had sent out an email to everyone about Sophie's fall, and several members wrote back to say they would be going by to see her.

"I think she might enjoy company even more once she gets home," Sarah suggested. She remembered Sophie talking about how lonesome she had been after her knee replacement. "I got used to having all those people around in the hospital, and my house seemed very empty," she had said.

Of course, now she has Timothy and Penny, she thought. *At least for now.*

* * * * *

Sarah had just returned from visiting with Sophie the next day and found Charles sitting at the kitchen table staring off into space. He was startled when she spoke to him and said, "I didn't hear you come in."

"Sorry if I startled you." She came up behind his chair and rubbed his tight neck muscles. "Are you okay?" she asked.

"John called today," he responded in a less than enthusiastic tone.

"And?"

"Well, he's talked with his friend in the FBI. Seymour hasn't been forthcoming. He told John he couldn't talk about the case, and that he hadn't been able to find out very much himself. He said they were keeping a tight lid on it. He did say one thing that may or may not be encouraging."

"May or may not be? What did he say?"

"Seymour said that all he can confirm is that the FBI is working with the U.S. Marshal's office and that this is a witness protection case. Your friend must have been in the program and has been very convincing with her new identity. I know you certainly thought that you knew her."

"Charles, I *do* know her. Are you thinking that her whole Amish history is just a ruse? Don't you remember when her father was dying, and she went up to see her family? Do you remember her stories about that trip? About sitting on the front porch with her brother and his wife because she wasn't allowed inside the house?"

"All I'm suggesting is …"

"What you're suggesting is that was all made up. Charles, I don't believe it. I could feel her pain when she told me that story."

"I know that you believe her …"

"Charles, I …" She couldn't finish her sentence. She was feeling angry with the FBI, the Chicago police, with whoever took her friend, and at that moment, with Charles as well.

"Honey, …" he began, trying to appease her.

"No, not now," she responded pulling away from him. "I'm going for a walk," she added, pulling on her sweater and grabbing Barney's leash.

Chapter 16

It had been two weeks since Ruth disappeared. Sarah had planned to work on one of her quilts, but she was feeling at loose ends. Ruth had been on her mind most of the time since Charles told her about the witness protection theory. She felt certain that Ruth was exactly who she said she was, but then she realized there could be something none of them knew about. When Caitlyn called and asked if she was free to go to the shelter to look at dogs, she was relieved.

"Caitlyn, that's exactly what I need today. What time does your father want to go?"

"Papa is teaching at the prison this morning, but he said I could go and just look if you were available to take me."

"I can't think of anything I'd rather do today. I'll pick you up in twenty minutes." Before leaving, she called Sophie to make sure she was okay. She got out of the hospital on schedule, but Tim had insisted she come stay with him and Penny for a few days. Sarah had offered to keep Emma, but Sophie was sure that the dog was worried about her, so Tim came by and picked her up. Sarah had to smile thinking about Timothy, Sophie, Penny, and two dogs nestled into that little bungalow that Tim was renting.

Sarah wrote a quick note to Charles, who was at the hardware store, telling him where she was going and suggesting that they go out to dinner that evening. Their relationship had felt strained the past couple of days, and Sarah knew she should break the ice. She recognized that her husband was just trying to help and that his many years with the police department had taught him to be suspicious of everyone involved in a crime, and to remove himself from his cases emotionally. But she *was* emotionally involved and would be until her friend was returned home.

As she pulled up in front of Andy's house, Caitlyn came running out and hopped into the car unable to contain her excitement. "We won't be able to bring one home today, will we?"

"No, your father will have to go back and fill out the application, and they'll also do a home visit."

"Why?" she asked in that whiny tone only a teenage girl can produce.

"Because they want to know the dog is going to a good home."

"We have a good home, don't we?" The tone was still there but improving.

"You certainly do. You have a loving home, and you have experience caring for dogs. You have the perfect home to offer a dog. By the way, be sure that your father puts my name and Sophie's down as references. They know both of us."

Caitlyn giggled with excitement as they pulled up in front of the shelter but became more subdued once they were inside. She approached the receptionist hesitantly and in a very serious tone said, "Hello. I'm Caitlyn Burgess, and I would like to adopt a dog."

The receptionist smiled and introduced a young man who had just entered the room. "This is Robert, our kennel manager. He'll show you the dogs available for adoption."

After talking with Sarah and Caitlyn for a few minutes to get an idea of what they were looking for, the young man opened the door to the kennel and escorted them down an aisle of barking dogs. Caitlyn looked overwhelmed. Sarah noticed she moved to the far side of the aisle when passing by the larger dogs. Sarah noticed a medium-sized dog that looked somewhat like her own Barney, and he was just as straggly looking as Barney had been when she brought him home. She wondered what this dog had gone through in his short life. Her heart went out to him.

Suddenly Caitlyn dropped to her knees in front of a small dog with mournful brown eyes and long orange-toned brown hair. The dog's tail began to wag, slowly at first but then enthusiastically. Caitlyn stuck her fingers through the wire, and the dog licked them affectionately.

"Look at this beautiful dog," Caitlyn cried. The sign said it was a red, long-haired dachshund.

Robert, the shelter manager, had remained with them and explained that the little dog had only been there for a day or two. "Her owner died last week, and the family couldn't keep the dog." He went on to explain that the family had flown in for their sister's funeral, but they both had busy jobs back in New York and didn't have enough time to care for a dog. "They were reluctant to give her up," he added, "but they didn't think they had any choice since she would be alone all day if they took her back to New York with them."

"That was a wise decision," Sarah responded. "Dogs are pack animals and can become very anxious and depressed when they're left alone too long."

"I assured them that this cute little dog would have a home in a matter of days. She's a lovely dog. Would you like for me to take her out so you can walk around with her?"

"Yes," Caitlyn responded enthusiastically. Although she was sixteen now, Sarah thought she could imagine what the younger Caitlyn could have been, a side the girl hadn't been able to experience in her very troubled past.

As Robert opened the door and snapped on the leash, the dog began to wag her entire body. "She looks so little from the front, but she's very long," Caitlyn commented still sitting on the floor as the dog walked into her arms.

"She's a dachshund. Some people call them a wiener dog," the kennel manager said.

Caitlyn laughed and held the dog's face between her hands. "You're no hot dog, are you?" she said lovingly. "What's her name?" she asked, turning to Robert.

"Her owner had named her Gretchen, but you could change it if you want. Lots of people do. She probably hasn't had much chance to learn her name anyway. I understand her owner had been sick for a long time."

"Gretchen?" Caitlyn repeated, looking doubtful. "I'm not sure she looks like a Gretchen." She repeated the name and the dog didn't respond. "Do you think she'd mind being named Sabrina? Her ears look like long curly hair around her face—she just looks like a Sabrina to me." Caitlyn cocked her head to the side and looked at the dog thoughtfully. "Sabrina?" she called, and the dog wiggled with excitement. "See? She likes it," Caitlyn announced excitedly.

As the two got to know one another, Robert and Sarah stepped back and talked about the adoption process. Sarah explained about how she got Barney. It was before Robert's time, but he thanked her for giving him a good home. Sarah asked about the dachshund and learned that she was only two years old.

"Can we take her home, Aunt Sarah? Please, please?" *That tone again.*

"Your dad will need to fill out the application like we talked about." Turning to the kennel manager, she asked, "Is there any way you can hold the dog for her?"

"I think these two are a perfect match. I'd be happy to hold little … Sabrina, is it?" he said smiling at Caitlyn. "When do you think her father could come in?"

"He's only working until noon today," Caitlyn said with excitement. "He'll come in right away, okay?"

"Okay, that's fine. I'll hold her for twenty-four hours." He excused himself and returned with a new sign that read: *Sabrina—Pending Adoption.* He took the dog out of Caitlyn's arms and placed her back in the kennel.

"Sorry, little girl," Caitlyn said reassuringly. "I have to go now, but I'll be back for you."

* * * * *

Sitting across the table from her handsome husband in the dimly lit restaurant, Sarah reached over and touched his hand. "I'm sorry I got so prickly the other day, Charles. I've thought about it, and I realize that you could be right, at least partially right. I don't believe she made up her stories about her parents, but that doesn't mean she wasn't involved in something she couldn't tell me about."

"It's okay, hon. I understand. She's been a good friend for several years, and I know how worried you are about her. For the FBI to be involved, I'd like to believe they're doing everything they can to find her, whatever the story is with her.

The waitress arrived with their dinner, and they set the issue aside and enjoyed a delicious meal of comfort food at their favorite Italian restaurant. Sarah told him about her trip to the shelter with Caitlyn and little Sabrina, and he told her about his frustrating trip to the hardware store where he was waited on by a kid who didn't know what a washer was. "He tried to send me to the appliance store."

As they walked in the door several hours later, Sarah saw the message light flashing. Seeing that it was Andy's number, she returned the call without listening to the message.

"Oh," Andy responded when he heard her voice. "That was Caitlyn calling you. I'll let her give you the news."

Moments later, Caitlyn came to the phone breathlessly. "She's here already," she said excitedly. "They let us bring her home."

"Already? You mean they did the home study today?"

"No, Aunt Sarah. Thanks to you and Aunt Sophie as references, they let us take her home today. They're coming out tomorrow, but they talked to Sophie already, and they said it was just a formality."

"How is she doing? Is she happy to be in her new home?" Sarah asked, knowing the answer already.

"She's so excited," Caitlyn responded. "She's checked out the whole house and is playing with her toys now."

"She has toys already?"

"Sure. We stopped at the pet store and got toys and food and a bed and … oh, and a tag with her name on it and our phone number like Barney and Emma have." Caitlyn's excitement was contagious as Sarah asked questions and laughed as she listened to the various antics little Sabrina was performing.

"Bring her over in a few days after she gets settled so she can meet Barney."

"Do you still have Emma?" Caitlyn asked sounding reluctant.

"No, she's back with Sophie."

"Okay then, I'll bring her over. I thought two dogs might be too much for her all at once." Sarah smiled at the protectiveness Caitlyn was already providing the little dog, and she wished there had been someone to protect Caitlyn during her childhood.

Later that night, the phone rang, and it was Charles' son, John. "I have some news for you and Sarah," he began, and Charles immediately put the call on speaker. Sarah sat down on the couch next to him.

"Yes, John. We need some news. What's happened?"

"I had a call from Seymour. He said there'd been a dramatic development. It seems they ran Ruth's picture through their facial recognition software."

"Ruth's face wasn't there was it?"

"No, actually it wasn't, however, they came up with someone else, a Tina Manchester."

"Who is that?" Sophie asked, looking bewildered.

"That's all I could find out for now, but I thought it was an interesting development. I immediately assumed it was your friend's alias, which would make sense if she'd been in witness protection, but Seymour's contact told him it wasn't actually a perfect match. Of course, your friend could have had some facial work done, I suppose."

"That's crazy," Sarah mumbled.

"It sometimes happens in the program, Sarah."

"This is becoming more and more outrageous," Sarah remarked as she stood up and walked across the room.

"It sure is," Charles responded frowning thoughtfully.

Turning back, Sarah said, "Ask him if she'd be in that database if she were in witness protection."

John, hearing her question, replied, "They wouldn't have intentionally been entered, but there are many ways to get your face in the files. I suppose they could have everyone with a driver's license in the database. This software is used worldwide now. We've used it in large crowds and stadiums, searching for potential criminals or terrorists. Mexico has even used it to detect voter fraud."

"*Curiouser and curiouser,*" Sarah muttered as she walked into the kitchen, leaving Charles to speak with his son. When she returned to the living room, she found her husband staring off into space.

"What is it?" she asked.

"This case keeps taking on strange turns. I wonder how Tina Manchester fits into it, assuming she even does."

Chapter 17

It was the morning of the third quilt club meeting since Ruth vanished. Sarah was pulling together odds and ends that she thought would work in her fidget quilt in addition to the few things she had picked up the previous day at the craft shop.

Suddenly, she had an idea, and she pulled out her laptop. Later when Charles came into the room, he found his wife with a very distressed look on her face. At first, she didn't seem to want to talk about it, but after some encouragement, she admitted that she needed his help.

"I hope you won't be upset with me, Charles, but I did a computer search on the name your son mentioned the other night, Tina Manchester."

"Why would I be upset with you? I was going to do that myself. What did you find?"

"Well, that's not the whole story. I did the search and got dozens of Tina Manchester's, but only one was in Chicago and this is the part I thought you might not like. I paid to get more information on her."

"That's fine, honey. You're detecting. What did you learn?"

"Nothing, because I suddenly lost my connection and when I went back in, I couldn't find her again."

"What do you mean?"

"All the other Tina Manchesters came up, but the one listed in Chicago was gone."

"Did you write down any of the information?"

"I did," she said, sounding relieved. "I have her social security number and her address."

"Here, let me try." He quickly confirmed that there was no one by that name in Chicago.

"This isn't the only way to skin a fish," Charles said, signing into a private criminal justice database.

A few minutes later he said, "There's no such social security number as that," he said frowning. "Are you sure you wrote it down right?"

"I'm positive. I checked it very carefully. Can you check the address?" Charles tried several other sources and finally said, "The woman doesn't exist, the social security number doesn't exist, and the house at that address is vacant."

"Charles, this is crazy. She existed ten minutes ago. Wait, she also had a DUI. Surely you can find her that way."

"Right," he responded and went into another database.

"No luck," Charles reported moments later. "I'll call Matt." Matthew Stokely was Charles' Lieutenant before he retired and a good friend. Unfortunately, his call resulted only in confirmation that there was no DUI and no record of a Tina Manchester in the system.

"Am I going crazy?" Sarah asked, confused by what had happened. "She was there twenty minutes ago, Charles, and fifteen minutes ago she disappeared from the face of the earth. It's like someone just erased her. ..."

"Ah, you may be on to something."

"What?" she asked, hoping for some logical explanation.

"Let me think about this, and I want to call my son again. I wonder if this Seymour Jackson would be willing to talk to me directly. I have some questions about how this whole thing works."

An hour later, Agent Jackson called Charles, having heard from John and agreed to speak with his father. John hadn't mentioned that his father was, in fact, retired. "Like I told your son, Detective Parker, there's very little I know about this case, and even less that I can talk about."

"I just want to ask one question."

"Okay, go ahead."

"When someone in the witness protection is moved to a new identity, what happens to the old identity?"

"Generally speaking, the old identity is totally erased. But that's all. . . ."

"Thank you, Agent. That's all I wanted to know." *Tina Manchester has been erased.*

* * * * *

It was difficult for Sarah to keep the strange turn of events to herself when she arrived at Stitches that evening, but she had promised not to tell anyone, including Sophie. She knew how hard that would be since Sophie could always tell when she was holding something back, so she was somewhat relieved when Tim called to say that Sophie didn't want to go to the meeting that night.

"Let's dump all our treasures in the middle of the table unless there's something you want to hold back to use yourself," Anna said. Everyone emptied their tote bags onto the table and the only thing held back was a little furry toy with a squeaker inside.

"I'm planning to make a little pocket for it and attach it by a cord so it doesn't get lost when the person pulls it out," Allison announced. "It actually belonged to our little boy, but he never played with it, and I ran it through the washer. Is that okay?"

"Lots of our things are used," Kimberly said as she emptied a bag of buttons onto the table along with a skein of multicolored yarn and assorted pieces of lace. "And I brought these keys as well. They're something everyone is familiar with. I thought they might inspire good memories."

Christina added a half-yard piece of brown faux-fur and a strip of white craft fur. "These will feel really good. I thought I might make a pocket out of a piece of the fur, but help yourselves to the rest." She cut herself a piece.

Sarah had purchased several yards of different types of fringe and several packages of rick rack.

"Here are some zippers from my stash of notions," Anna said as she placed a dozen zippers in different sizes and colors on the table. Anna had also cut eight-and-a-half-inch squares of various fabrics: solids, tone-on-tones, bright fabrics, and some with familiar designs. They had decided to use nine squares sewn together in three rows of three to make the quilt approximately twenty-four inches by twenty-four inches finished.

Delores arrived late, explaining that she had been taking care of her granddaughter's foster child and had to wait for her to get home from work, but when she dumped her tote bag on the table, everyone squealed with delight. There were at least a dozen little furry animals, a half-dozen small rag dolls, ribbons, and several dozen plastic rings for attaching items to the quilt. "Where did you get all these things?" Caitlyn asked.

"My grandson works in one of those dollar-type stores, and he was able to get these at a discount."

"The rag dolls, too? I've never seen such small ones, and they even have hair."

"Actually, I made those," Delores responded. "I thought we could make little dresses for them."

Frank came in late, as he often did because of his job. He was carrying a large paper bag and looked hesitant when everyone turned to greet him. "I don't know if you'll want to use this. I told my grandmother what we were doing, and she said if we put flannel on the back, it wouldn't slip off the person's lap."

"Frank," Sarah responded excitedly. "What an excellent idea."

He reached into his bag and pulled out several yards of solid blue flannel. "Grandma said we can have this. She said she didn't need it."

"Please thank her for us, Frank," Anna said. "This will be perfect. I'll cut it now."

"If everyone will choose the nine pieces of fabric you want to use, I'd be happy to sit at the machine and start stitching them together," Sarah offered. With Ruth and Tina Manchester on her mind, she didn't feel very creative but knew she could sit and sew straight lines with no problem. "Put your name on your pile so I can get it back to you."

Within minutes, she had her first pile to work on, and soon all of the others were piled on the table next to her.

She pinned the quilter's name on each one when it was finished and set it aside.

"I think we should layer our finished quilt top with batting and a back before we start adding things," Anna said as she came back into the work room with a pile of flannel backs. "That way our stitches will go all the way through and make it more stable."

"Good idea, especially since they won't be quilted."

"Maybe we should be quilting them," Delores said. "How about if I sit over here, and as Sarah finishes stitching a top she can pass it to me, and I'll layer it and straight-line quilt through the middle of the blocks."

"What about the binding?"

"You can add that yourself when it's finished. I know some people want to add fringe and Sarah was talking about prairie points."

"I was thinking about turning mine so it wouldn't need binding," Allison said.

"That's a good idea, too," Delores responded. "Get your fabric top from Sarah if you want to add the batting and back and turn it. After you finish, bring it to me if you want, and I'll quilt it."

"Okay, let's get our sweatshop going." Sarah handed Delores her first piece ready for quilting while everyone else rummaged through the decorations, choosing items for their own fidget quilt.

By the end of the meeting, everyone had a few things attached to their fidget quilts and were proudly showing them off. "Do you want to take them home," Anna asked, "Or do you want to leave them here?"

"I suggest," Sarah began, "that we leave everything here and pick up where we left off next week. This is fun to do together. Do you have room for all this, Anna?"

"I certainly do." She left the room and returned with a large box and everyone carefully stacked their quilts inside followed by all their materials.

"I'd like to take one of Delores' little dolls home to make it a dress," Allison said.

"Oh, I want to do that too," Caitlyn chimed in. Turning to Sarah, she whispered, "Will you help me?"

"Yes, and please grab one for me. We'll do them together."

As she was driving home, her mind went back to Ruth. She felt guilty about the fact that she had become so absorbed in the activities of the evening that she hadn't thought once about her friend. But she knew that's what Ruth would have wanted her to do, and she smiled when she thought how happy her friend would be when she returned and saw that her idea had been such a success. *When she returns*, Sarah repeated the thought, but her smile began to fade.

* * * * *

"Sophie, how are you feeling this morning?" Sarah asked when her friend answered the phone the next morning. "I hope I didn't wake you up."

"I've been up since daybreak feeling bright-eyed and bushy-tailed," Sophie responded. "I'm just happy to be home with my Emma." She had returned to her own home the previous day and was getting around on her crutches. "What are you up to this morning?"

"I want to take a road trip. Are you up for five or six hours in the car?"

"As long as we can stop for a meal or two, I'd love to get out in the world. I'm tired of being treated like an invalid. What are you up to?"

"I want to do some detecting."

"Does Charles know what you're doing?"

"No, but I fully intend to tell him *after* I do it, that is. Here's the thing." Sarah told her friend about Tina Manchester and how all reference to her on the internet had vanished, including a DUI from her police records. "I want to drive up to Chicago and talk to her neighbors. Maybe someone knows where she went."

"What does this woman have to do with Ruth?" Sophie asked.

"I don't know. Maybe nothing. I just know that when the FBI used their facial recognition software to search for Ruth, this woman came up. It just might be a clue."

Sophie held the phone for a few moments without speaking. Finally, she let out a deep sigh and said, "Sarah, I'm about to be the sensible one here, and don't you ever tell anyone. I wouldn't want that to get around, but here goes: Don't do it."

"What? You're always ready for an adventure."

"Not this kind of adventure," Sophie responded. "I've seen what's been happening, and I've listened, and everything I've heard makes me think this isn't some everyday crime. I believe we're talking about some very dangerous people— people connected to things we don't want to know about."

Sarah sighed. "I suppose you're right, but …"

"Just stay out of it."

"But I want to do something to help Ruth," Sarah groused. "I feel so helpless, and I thought I might find out something from this woman's old neighbors. There just might be some connection."

"Sarah, let's think about this. If you moved tomorrow, your address would still be on the internet, along with your age and your associates, whatever that means, right?"

"Your point?"

"My point," Sophie responded emphatically, "is that we're talking about people who can not only make a woman disappear, they can erase all evidence of her existence. Stay out of it, my friend. I don't want to lose you too!"

"I guess you're right, but someone needs to be checking this out."

"It sounds to me like a job for that cute detective up there, what's his name?"

"Jake?" Sarah responded. "Jake Krakowski." She could hear Sophie's mischievous smile.

"Ah, yes, Jake. Why don't you call him and tell him everything you learned and suggest he check out the neighbors."

"Well, I don't know if he can do that, Sophie. He told Charles that his department had been taken off the case. The FBI took over, remember?"

"I know, but if you were to ask him to do this one teeny little favor for you …" Sophie responded, her voice dripping with innuendo.

"Sophie, stop that. I'm a married woman and old enough to be his mother."

"But Charles did say he thought the detective was sweet on you, right?"

"Sophie, stop!" Sarah grumbled. She was glad they were on the phone, and her friend couldn't see her blushing.

"But I think you might be on to something here," she added. "He could, at least, check it out."

"Call me after you talk to him."

"I will. Thanks, Sophie, I promise that I will never tell anyone how sensible you have become."

"I appreciate that."

Now where did I put that number? She looked in her purse, but it wasn't there. Thinking back, she remembered that he had handed her his card as they were saying goodbye in the café, and she had slipped it into her jacket pocket.

Sarah dialed the number, hoping she wasn't doing the wrong thing. The phone rang eight or nine times, and she was prepared to leave a message when suddenly he picked up. "Krakowski, here." Sarah identified herself and started to explain why she was calling when the detective interrupted her.

"Sarah," he said more warmly than one would expect from a police detective. "I was hoping I'd hear from you,"

Could Charles possibly be right?

* * * * *

"No, honey, I'm not upset with you for calling Jake. In fact, I wanted to ask him to question the neighbors myself, but I knew he couldn't do it officially. I'd even thought about going up there myself."

Sarah didn't tell him she had considered doing the same thing herself.

"What did he say?" Charles asked.

"He was very interested when I told him that all references to Tina Manchester had vanished from the internet. I even told him about the DUI, and he started to say something about the FBI but didn't finish it. I think he'd say more to you. Maybe when he calls back, you can talk to him."

"I think he'd rather talk to you," Charles replied waggling his eyebrow.

"Don't start," she responded trying to look offended. "What do you want for lunch?"

Chapter 18

The phone was ringing when Sarah came in from the backyard with Barney. "Sophie, good morning," she answered, seeing her friend's name on the phone.

"I have some news, possibly good news," Sophie reported.

"We all need some good news, Sophie. What is it?"

"Tim came over last night and said he and Penny had been talking." As promised, the day Sophie left the hospital and went to stay with Tim, she had announced a family meeting. She told Sarah later that Penny had cried and pleaded, and Timothy had listened. Sophie had also said that her son explained why he was considering the job, and she could understand. "He's a young man," she had said. "He wants to be productive."

"So what's this possible good news?" Sarah asked.

"He talked to the recreation department at the community center up the street about starting up a baseball team for seniors. It seems we have a retired orthopedic surgeon living here who specialized in sports medicine. They contacted him, and he's willing to work with Timmy to make sure these old guys don't get hurt."

"Sophie, that's wonderful. Is he going to stay then?"

"He said he's considering it. He can see what this potential move is doing to Penny."

"I'm glad he's willing to listen to her. It must be hard to suddenly be the parent of a teenager."

"He's becoming a really good dad," Sophie replied proudly. "He also found an online degree course in Safety, and he's thinking of enrolling so he can be considered for local jobs."

"Safety? What do they teach?"

"I didn't understand it all, but he mentioned construction safety, and I guess workplace safety in general. It's actually what he was doing in Alaska on the pipeline. I guess this class would just upgrade his skills and maybe broaden his knowledge so he could work in other settings."

"Sophie, it sounds like he just might stay."

"Maybe, and if he does, we'll have Charles to thank. Timmy keeps quoting things Charles said to him. He respects Charles, and I think he's beginning to see him as a father figure."

"Charles is a good man," Sarah said with a loving smile that Sophie couldn't see, but she could hear it.

"He is," Sophie agreed. "And as far as this move goes, we'll just have to wait and see, but I know he has to make a decision soon. He has to either leave for Altoona or let them know he isn't coming."

"So what are you up to today?" Sarah asked.

"To tell you the truth, ever since you suggested driving to Chicago, I've been stir crazy. I'd love to go somewhere— not Chicago, mind you, but somewhere. Any ideas?"

"It should be somewhere you won't have to walk much." Sophie would be on her crutches for another few weeks. "By the way, how's physical therapy going?"

"It's fine. I have a young therapist who seems to understand about old folks. She's taking it slow, but she said walking around was a good thing to build up my strength. How about the quilt museum in Hamilton? I'd like to see some appliqué now that I'm getting into this."

Hamilton was only forty-five minutes away and would be an easy trip as long as Sophie could walk. "In fact, Sophie, they have wheelchairs there if you need a rest. Let's do it."

They spent the next few hours visiting in the car and walking through the museum. Sarah had only given cursory glances at the appliquéd quilts in the past since she was making pieced quilts, and she enjoyed the careful examination that Sophie was giving them.

They were both impressed by the Baltimore Album Quilts. Sophie read the sign aloud which explained that they originated in the 1840s in Baltimore and were made by the more prosperous quilters who were able to use new fabrics rather than scraps. Each very intricate block was unique, the sign said, and often designed by the quilter herself. "I could never design one myself," Sophie commented, "but I'd like to make one, maybe a little simpler than these."

"There are patterns for making a Baltimore Album Quilt with templates for the appliqué. I think Ruth has a book in her shop. Let's stop there on our way home."

When they got to the shop later that afternoon, Delores had just finished a class and was ringing up one of her student's purchases. When she was finished, Sophie told her what she wanted to do, and Delores showed her the book. Sophie's face fell as she thumbed through the instructions. "This looks very complicated," she said, looking disappointed.

"I was thinking about starting a Baltimore Album class next month," Delores responded. "I have one other customer who's interested. If you want to learn, that will make two, and a few others might sign up."

"I just might sign up too," Sarah said, eager to get her mind on something new.

"Do you want to buy the book today so you can start getting familiar with the quilt?" she asked Sophie.

As Delores headed for the book section, Sarah called after her saying, "Pick up one for me, too, please."

They paid for their books, and Delores wrote a note to Anna, asking her to advertise the class and to order more books. "This will be fun," she added as she placed the books in a bag.

All three women were excited about the possibility of the class, but their enthusiasm was diminished by the realization that Ruth was not there to enjoy this moment with them. She always loved it when her customers were about to learn something new.

* * * * *

"I heard from Jake this morning," Charles announced as Sarah walked into his den.

"Oh? Did he go to Tina's neighborhood?"

"He did, and he learned zilch. No one knew her personally, but they saw her come and go every day, seemingly going to work. They never saw visitors and they never had an opportunity to talk with her."

"But she went to work? Did he find out where?"

"No. He talked to her landlord who said he accepted her without an application. An outfit called Browning Associates had said they needed a furnished place for an employee, and he agreed to accept her without a lease. The company vouched for her and paid a year in advance."

"Did Jake talk to Browning?"

"Couldn't. No such company."

"What?"

"But Jake had a good question for us."

"What's that?"

"He asked why we are pursuing this as a lead. This Tina person is obviously not Ruth and apparently had no connection to Ruth. I told him her picture came up on a facial recognition database when they fed Ruth's picture in."

"He said it looks like a coincidence, and I'm inclined to agree. I think you and I got sidetracked. I'm sure the FBI knew better."

"We were just hopeful...." Sarah said sadly. But then brightening up, she added, "But I have some good news on another topic."

"What's that?"

"Tim is considering staying here." She told him about the possibility of a senior citizen's baseball team, and that Tim is exploring online classes to upgrade his skills in case he decides to look for a job locally. Sophie said she thinks you may have had a big influence on her son."

"This is good news. I hope it works out for them." Charles sighed and turned back to his computer screen looking troubled. "I guess we should forget about the elusive Tina Manchester and come up with a new idea for finding Ruth."

"I wouldn't dismiss Ms. Manchester too soon," Sarah responded.

Chapter 19

An isolated cabin outside Chicago ...

As the freight train rumbled past within yards of the rundown shack, it shook the walls causing bits of the deteriorating ceiling to crumble and fall to the concrete floor. Ruth lay on the cot where she spent most of her time since they brought her to this lonely place. Three times a day someone lifted the access cover and came down the steps with a meager meal which was wordlessly placed next to her. Her restraints had been removed, and she'd been told never to make a sound. She remained silent. Her only hope was to stay alive.

The men rarely spoke to her and offered no explanation for her abduction.

Ruth looked around the room and memorized every niche and corner. She memorized every sound and every word she heard. She kept track of every morsel of food she ate and every odor she smelled. It was all she had to do, and she felt that it would help her maintain her sanity and, if anyone ever found her, perhaps these memories could lead them to the men who had taken her.

For distraction, she sometimes walked for hours around the room, counting her steps and estimating distance. *One mile.* She even ventured partway up the steps once to see if she could hear what the men were saying, but she discovered they were speaking another language, perhaps Spanish.

And she slept, sometimes all day.

Sometimes she went over the whole thing in her mind, trying to understand ... trying to remember all the details.

I was preparing to unlock my van, she remembered, when the man grabbed me from behind and covered my mouth. He forced me into the van parked near mine. I tried to resist, but he was strong. There was another man in the van. He drove, and the one who grabbed me sat in the back next to me. Once we were out of the parking lot, they stopped, blindfolded me, and tied my hands together at the wrist.

I wanted to know what they wanted, but I couldn't ask, and they never said. I tried to be compliant, hoping they would let me go. Hoping they wouldn't kill me.

They drove for about an hour, part of the time through traffic and then on what seemed to be a winding country road. When they stopped, the man sitting next to me pulled me out of the van and took off my blindfold. He left the gag and restraints in place. I recognized nothing.

The two men were rough and crude talking, but they didn't hurt me. Once we got inside, I saw a third man sitting at the table. He looked surprised and said, "You guys are crazy. Why did you pick her up?" and one of the men, the one with a long scar down the side of his face, said that the boss had ordered them to. The third man shook his head in disgust. "Big mistake," he muttered.

One of the men kicked a rug aside exposing a trap door. He led me down the steps into the cellar. There was one small window near the ceiling probably at ground level. I quickly looked around for something to stand on to reach the window, but there was nothing. There were two cots near the window and a portable commode in the corner. They left me there, wordlessly.

I sat down on the side of the bed and wept, but I couldn't wipe my tears away nor blow my nose since my wrists were bound, so I forced myself to calm down.

Later the third man came downstairs. He removed all my restraints and said that if I remained completely silent, he'd leave them off. He seemed kind. I started to ask why they had brought me here, but he stopped me and threatened to tie me up again. "Don't speak or yell," he said firmly.

When the man was ready to leave, he reminded me to remain quiet, and as he walked up the wooden steps, he looked back at me and said, "Don't worry, no one is going to hurt you. Just stay perfectly silent down here and you'll be okay."

I nodded and didn't speak. He smiled and left.

Time dragged on, and because of the small window, Ruth was able to tell day from night. They brought her food. She slept. Time passed. Sometimes when she opened her eyes during the night, she would see that the kind man was sleeping in the other bed. At first, it frightened her, but he was always gone when she woke up. It began to make her feel safe.

One day he brought her four books and laid them on the bed. He told her his name was Julio and that she shouldn't worry. Ruth almost spoke, but he gently shook his head. She began to think she just might get out someday.

Chapter 20

"Hi, Aunt Sarah. Are you busy?"

"Good morning, Caitlyn," Sarah responded, putting her coffee cup in the dishwasher and sitting down to talk. "I'm not busy at all," she responded. "I just finished the breakfast dishes and got Charles on his way. He went over to help Tim do some career planning."

"I know," Caitlyn responded excitedly. "Penny just called me, and she said her dad has been talking seriously about turning down the job in Altoona. She's so happy. Thank you, Aunt Sarah. I knew you could fix it."

"I didn't do anything, Caitlyn, except get people talking to each other. I think it helped for them to understand each other's feelings about the move. And Charles talked to Timothy about some alternatives. Tim hasn't made any definite decisions yet. I hope Penny isn't getting her hopes up too soon."

"Penny said he sounds pretty serious."

There was a pause in the conversation, and Sarah wondered why Caitlyn was calling. To help her along she said, "So what are you doing today?"

"Well," she responded hesitantly. "I was wondering if you might want to start on the doll dresses. But it's okay if you're too busy."

"It's a perfect time, Caitlyn. And bring Sabrina along. I'm eager to see her again, and I know Barney's going to love her."

"Really? I can bring her?"

"Of course. She's welcome to come here anytime. You know, dogs are pack animals, and they love getting together with their own kind. How's she doing, by the way?"

"She's such a doll. She made herself right at home, and she was already trained. She barks at the back door when she needs to go out. I have to take her on a leash, but Papa is going to have a fence put up out back. The guy's coming over today to measure and let him know what it's going to cost."

"Has Sabrina been to the vet?"

"Yep. We took her right away, and he said she's in fine shape. He did tell us to be very careful with her back. I guess dachshunds can have serious back problems, and she isn't supposed to jump from high places like the couch and the bed. We got carpeted steps for her to use by the couch, and Papa put a dog bed in my room. He said Sabrina shouldn't get up on the bed."

"Barney has his own bed too," Sarah responded, but she wondered if it wasn't hard for Caitlyn. She remembered that Barney had slept with her when she took care of him, and Caitlyn had been very animated when she talked about how she loved snuggling with a dog.

"But Sabrina wants to sleep with me," Caitlyn added. "Do you think it's okay? I can lift her up and down."

"You should talk to your dad about that," Sarah responded, not wanting to get in the middle. "So, when do you want to come over?"

"Would it be okay to come in about an hour? I haven't finished my chores, but if I hurry, I'll be done by then."

"That's just fine. I'll have my chores done by then too." Sarah was smiling to herself as she hung up, thinking what a good job these two men were doing with their girls. Timothy and Andy both found themselves single dads late in life, and they had both managed to excel at their new responsibilities.

Thinking about Penny, Sarah picked up the phone and called her. "I was just thinking that since Charles is over there talking to your dad, you just might like to come over here."

"Sure, I guess," she responded.

"Caitlyn and Sabrina are on their way, and you can bring Blossom." Penny's tone changed completely from mild indifference to unbridled excitement. "Dad," Sarah heard her cry. "Can I go to Aunt Sarah's, please, please?" She could hear Timothy in the background, and it sounded like he agreed. Charles came to the phone to say he'd drive them over.

"Thanks, hon," he said. "We're doing some serious planning over here. Penny was already looking bored." Sarah told him what was going on at their house and encouraged him to stay with Tim as long as it took.

By the time Caitlyn arrived, Sarah and Penny had all the fabric scraps out, and the three began talking about how to make the dresses. "Why don't we make a simple little pinafore?" Sarah suggested.

Neither girl was familiar with the term, so Sarah made a quick sketch. "That's sort of like an apron," Caitlyn said.

"Yes, and it will be simple to make." Sarah and Caitlyn told Penny about the fidget quilts and how the dolls would be used. Sarah pulled out the quilt Ruth had purchased at the show, and Penny was fascinated with it.

"This would be good for kids, too," Caitlyn suggested.

"I think that's where the idea came from," Sarah responded. "I believe they're sometimes used with autistic children."

"I want to work with children when I grow up," Penny said.

Thinking that Penny might feel left out of the project, Sarah reached into her cabinet and pulled out a small stuffed animal she had purchased for Barney but had decided it was too small for him. "How would you like to make a dress for this little kitten?" she asked, and Penny clapped her hands together.

"Oh, thank you," she squealed. Sarah had to remind herself that Penny was fourteen. She was brought up in such isolation, that she displayed the innocence of a much younger child.

They spent the next couple of hours on their projects, and Penny proudly lined them up on the kitchen table as Sarah prepared lunch. "Let's take the dogs for a walk after lunch," Caitlyn suggested. It was a warm spring day, a nice day for a walk.

"Why don't we walk over to Sophie's and invite Emma to go with us," Sarah suggested before she realized that was quite a few dogs for them to manage.

About that time, Charles walked in from the garage. "Hi, girls," he said. "Penny, I think your dad might have some news for you."

"Don't you think you should wait and let her father tell her?" Sarah interjected before he had a chance to say too much.

"Oh, he will," Charles said with a wide grin as he turned and looked back into the garage. "He's right behind me."

Moments later, Timothy stepped into the kitchen with a Cheshire cat grin on his face.

"What is it, Daddy?" Penny asked as she reached for Blossom, who was already attacking her father's ankles and untying his shoe strings.

Simultaneously, Caitlyn grabbed Sabrina, who was heading for Timothy, excitedly whining and barking as if she were greeting a long lost friend when in fact they'd never met.

Barney lay on his mat on the kitchen floor, taking it all in and yawning. *These youngsters*, he seemed to be thinking.

"So, Dad, what?"

"I called Altoona and told them we won't be coming. We're staying right where we are," he announced with a wink. Moments later Penny was in his arms while all three dogs jumped on him with excitement. The dogs may not have known what they were excited about, but Penny sure did.

Sarah smiled at Charles and nodded. *Sometimes it pays to be a busybody.*

* * * * *

They were already in bed when the phone rang. Sarah was almost asleep, and Charles was already dozing. "I'll get it," she said, but Charles had already reached for the phone.

"Hello?"

"Dad, it's John. I hope it's not too late."

"It's fine. Is everyone okay?"

"We're all fine. I just had some information for you. I had a call tonight from Seymour. There's been another development."

Charles sat up and reached for the lamp. "What's happened?" he asked as he put the phone on speaker so Sarah could listen.

"He swore me to secrecy, Dad. He knew I'd tell you, but it can't go any farther."

"Sarah's right here, son. . . ."

"Oh, of course, Sarah can know, but no one else, especially Ruth's family. We don't want to get their hopes up. In fact, this information may not lead to anything good."

"What is it?" Sarah asked, impatient to know what had happened.

"The FBI made a connection when they began looking into this Tina Manchester. It seems she was, and I guess still is, in the Witness Protection Program."

"That would explain her sudden disappearance from the radar," Charles commented. "But what does that have to do with Ruth?"

"Remember the similarity in their looks? Tina Manchester, you'll remember, came up when they ran Ruth Weaver's picture through the facial recognition software."

"Yes, but what does this mean for Ruth?" Sarah asked.

"Sarah is asking ..." Charles began, but John interrupted him.

"I heard her. Sarah, what this means is they've finally found a possible explanation for why she was taken."

"I don't understand. ..." she responded.

"Let him finish," Charles said, gently laying his hand on her arm.

"They're going on the assumption that Ruth may have been kidnapped by mistake."

"By mistake?" Sarah cried. "Do they know who took her?"

"They have an idea, at least of who *might* be behind it."

"And who is that?" Charles asked.

"Seymour didn't want to share any details, but he ultimately mentioned a Dante Ybarra. This is one bad dude."

"Have they questioned him?"

"I don't know, but I confirmed today the guy's been in prison for some twenty years with three life sentences to go."

"So it couldn't be him," Sarah said with a degree of relief.

"These guys have outside connections," Charles responded to her, then to his son he asked, "So what's next?"

"We wait, and remember, this is just a theory. This may not be the explanation at all, but it's the closest thing to a lead they've had since her disappearance, at least as far as we know."

Sarah reached for the phone. "John, what are her chances if Ybarra's people are the ones who took her?"

"These guys are bottom feeders, Sarah. But remember, we don't know that's who has her. It's just the first piece of information we've been able to get out of the FBI. I will tell you this. Seymour assured me the agency is taking this very seriously. They're pulling out all the stops." Sarah thanked him and handed the phone back to Charles. She left the room to give her husband private time with his son, thinking there might be more information John just didn't want to share in front of her.

When Charles finished and came looking for his wife, he found her in the kitchen with a cup of herbal tea. "Did he have anything else to say?" she asked.

"No, just speculation and we don't need to go there."

"I agree." She stood, and he wrapped her in his arms.

"Remember, you can't tell anyone about this," Charles said softly as he held her.

"I wouldn't want anyone else to hear it. It's bad enough that we heard it," she responded.

Dante Ybarra, she repeated the name to herself. Charles felt her shiver and held her close.

Chapter 21

Sarah felt sad as she approached the chapel. She hadn't been to church since Ruth disappeared, yet she knew this was where she needed to be. The most recent news from Seymour had hit her hard. She had to face the reality that her friend might never come home.

The sanctuary was empty when she arrived. Sarah chose a seat in the back and lowered her head. Tears threatened to flow, but she sat quietly and allowed herself to experience the feeling of peace that she could always count on when she was in this sacred place.

She hadn't gone to the village chapel where she and Charles had been going since they met. She had instead driven across town to the church she had attended with Jonathan and the children—the church she had thought would be a part of their family throughout their lives. But instead it became the place for Jonathan's funeral and again for her young grandson. She hadn't been back since she moved to Cunningham Village.

She was startled when she felt a gentle hand on her shoulder but smiled when she looked into the kind eyes of

Pastor John. "Sarah," he said softly and motioned for her to follow him to this chamber.

When she left an hour later, she had shared her every fear and he had listened with gentle understanding. He prayed with her, and for the first time in weeks, she felt hope.

"And," she said aloud as she was driving home, "I know exactly what I will do." Charles wasn't home when she arrived. She poured a glass of iced tea, grabbed her computer glasses, and headed for Charles' den. She turned on his computer and did a Google search on the name Dante Ybarra. She smiled when she realized the name no longer frightened her.

An hour or so later she heard her husband coming in the back door. "I'm in here," she shouted. "Come see what I found."

Before he reached the room, he heard his out-of-date printer grinding away. "What's all this?"

"Meet one Dante Ybarra, better known among his friends and enemies as 'The Barracuda.' "

Charles saw the old sparkle in his wife's eyes and couldn't help asking, "What's happened to you?" He knew she'd been trying to stay strong, but, especially after Seymour's call, she seemed to be feeling the strain.

"Just a little refueling," she responded cryptically. "Look at this." She handed him a printout of a Texas newspaper.

He sat down and read about the arrest of a drug lord operating a cartel out of a small border town in Texas. Dante Ybarra, The Barracuda, and two of his lieutenants were arrested, along with several of his low-level falcons.

"When was this?" Charles asked, skipping ahead looking for a date.

"The trial was twenty-two years ago, and the daughter and wife of Malcolm Bradley, one of his lieutenants, were the primary witnesses." Sarah handed him another few pages. "This leads up to the trial."

"The wife could testify against Ybarra but not her husband," he said thoughtfully.

"I know," Sarah responded. "It looks like the daughter, Laura Bradley, was the state's primary witness against Ybarra. She was twenty-five at the time. Take a look at this," she said handing him another newspaper clipping. "This was from the trial."

"He was found guilty on all charges," he said.

She handed him an article with a frightening courtroom picture of Ybarra taken the day he was found guilty. "This next article came out several weeks later and reported that he was sentenced to three consecutive life sentences for the murders of three members of a rival cartel."

Charles frowned as he studied the articles, going back occasionally to a previous sheet.

"Read this one," Sarah said, handing him another printout. "This was another article that came out the day of sentencing." She turned around and watched Charles as he read the reporter's description of Ybarra's reaction to the judge's decision.

Looking directly at the state's witness with an ugly, threatening sneer, Ybarra snarled, "You'll die for this." It took three guards to drag The Barracuda out of the courtroom. In a later interview, Ms. Bradley said that testifying against her father was the hardest thing she had every done, but as far as Ybarra was concerned, she hated

him and was sorry they hadn't sent him to the gas chamber.
"He was responsible for my brother's death and ruined my
father's life," the young woman said.

"So her father worked for Ybarra," Charles said, "and
she testified against both of them. What happened to her
father?"

"He died in prison five years later."

"And this brother she mentions?"

"Drugs, it says somewhere here," Sarah responded,
shuffling back through the sheets.

"So what are you thinking?" he asked her, still looking at
the last article.

"That our Tina Manchester is Laura Bradley," she
responded, "and in witness protection."

"I agree, but where does that leave Ruth?"

"I have no idea," she responded, "but I'll bet we now
know just about as much as the FBI knows. How's that for
detecting?" she asked, looking proud of her efforts.

"You did great," he responded, knowing how much she
enjoyed playing amateur detective. "Did you look at this
picture of Laura Bradley?" he asked, picking up a printout
that had fallen to the floor.

"I sure did. And I know what you're thinking. That's
probably what Ruth would have looked like back then."

"Yes, it is," he agreed. "And you are totally certain Laura
and Ruth are not one and the same."

"Don't start that again, Charles. Ruth has a history that
we all know about. However, Laura and Tina are probably
one and the same."

"True. And did you do a Google search on Laura Bradley?" he asked, already knowing the answer.

"I sure did."

"And?"

"She vanished from the face of the earth the day after the trial. She no longer exists," Sarah responded, "thanks to the magic of witness protection, I assume."

"Just like Tina," he responded.

"So now what?" Sarah asked, pushing back from the computer.

"I have no idea," Charles responded. "Lunch perhaps?"

Chapter 22

It was the fourth meeting of the Friday Night Quilters without Ruth, and Sarah dreaded facing her friends, and especially Ruth's sister Anna, not being able to tell them this latest piece of information. She hoped that the FBI would be able to find Ruth now that they had somewhat of a lead, but she couldn't share this information, not even with Sophie.

She had just pulled up in front of Sophie's house and was starting to get out of the car when she saw Sophie hobbling toward her. "Where are your crutches?" Sarah called out before her friend had even reached the car.

"Stop nagging. It's been three weeks, and that's as long as Dr. Dean said I had to use them." Sophie struggled to get into the car and pulled the seatbelt across her pudgy middle.

"Okay," Sarah responded. "First of all, Dr. Dean said 'three or four weeks,' and second of all, it's only been two weeks."

"You're such a stickler for details," Sophie complained. "Start the car. I don't want to be late."

Sarah sighed, realizing her friend would do exactly what she wanted. On the way, they talked again about the fidget quilts and Sarah told her friend what they would be doing that night.

"But I don't have a quilt to put things on, and I don't know how to make one."

"Well, before I knew how medically noncompliant you were going to be, I made one for you. It's in that bag on the floor by your feet."

Sophie's face lit up as she pulled the small quilt out and looked at it. Sarah had used bright colors because she knew Sophie would like them but had used muted fabrics for her own.

"What are these other things?" Sophie asked, pulling out the two dolls and the kitten. "Caitlyn and I brought the dolls home and made the little dresses for them. The kitten is for you. Penny did that one and wanted you to have it for your quilt."

"Oh," Sophie responded with emotion. "That was so sweet of her. I love the little apron she's wearing."

"We talked about making little pockets on the quilt to put the dolls in."

"I can do that. I'll sew it on by hand. What else shall I add to it?" Since Sophie had missed the past few meetings, she hadn't seen all the supplies the members had contributed.

"You'll have your choice. We have enough for everyone: ribbons, buttons, zippers, rick rack, and beads. You'll have lots to choose from."

"Have you heard from John?" Sophie asked abruptly, and Sarah looked away, knowing her friend could read her face. "What's the matter? You know something, don't you?"

"John called to say they may have a lead, but we just have to wait. Let's not talk about it tonight, okay? Let's just have fun."

"Humph," Sophie responded, knowing there was more to be said, but she decided to let her friend off the hook.

When they walked into the shop, they were surprised to find several members quietly sitting around the work table deeply engrossed in their work. "Hi, girls," Delores said, greeting them without looking up. "Come see what we discovered."

Sarah pulled out their chairs and sat down across from Delores. "Here, try to pull this off," the woman said, passing her mini quilt with a row of beads on a cord attached at both ends so the user could move the beads back and forth."

"I don't want to pull it off," Sarah replied as she gently pulled.

"You can't. I stitched it on with this," she said, holding up a container of dental floss.

"How clever," Sarah responded, "but how did you get that thick stuff through your needle?"

"I used beading needles. I brought a few in, and everyone is welcome to use them and help yourself to the floss. Just be sure to return the needles. I'm making jewelry for all the girls in my family for Christmas."

"You're planning Christmas in May?" Sophie remarked.

"I sure am. I'm making necklaces for all the girls: my daughters, my daughter-in-laws, my grandchildren, every female in the family, and even for a couple of my close friends. That takes time."

"I'm duly impressed," Sophie responded, "and, by the way, I consider myself one of your closest and dearest friends." Everyone at the table laughed and shook their heads. *Sophie's back.*

"We can always count on Sophie to lighten things up," Kimberly announced as she held up her little quilt. "How do you like this?"

"I love it," Sarah responded, followed by comments from everyone including Anna, who had just come in from the storage room carrying a few more items she had found around the shop.

Myrtle arrived next, and Frank was right behind her, making his usual apologies for being late.

"It's never a problem, Frank," Anna assured him. "We know you work on Fridays."

It turned out to be a very quiet meeting as everyone worked diligently on their individual fidget quilts. During the last hour, they began talking more, asking one another's advice about what else they should attach.

"Oh, I almost forgot," Sophie announced. "When I was having physical therapy last week, I was talking with the head nurse from the Alzheimer's unit, and I told her about our quilts. She thinks they would be great for her patients, and she asked if she could have a couple to try them out."

"Yes," everyone responded at once.

"Is this the nursing home at Cunningham Village?"

"Yes, it's right by my house, and I go for physical therapy there three times a week. I'd be happy to take them," Sophie added.

"We'll have two or three finished by the next meeting," Delores said. "I'm taking mine home to bind it."

"Mine doesn't need binding," Christina said. "I turned it before Delores quilted it last week, so mine will be finished tonight."

"Mine, too," Kimberly added, "so that's two you can take with you tonight and let us know what she says next week."

"Good for you two," Allison remarked. "I wish I'd done that. It's going to be awkward sewing the binding on with all these things attached."

"Will you help me with my binding?" Caitlyn whispered to Sarah, who assured her she would.

As they were packing their projects away for the week, Christine and Kimberly passed their completed fidget quilts to Sophie to take to the nursing home. "Oh, wait, I wanted to get a picture of mine," Kimberly said as she pulled out her phone.

"Take one of mine, too," Christina added. "I want to show them to Ruth when she gets home." Sarah thought about the fact that she said it as if Ruth were just away on vacation and was expected back soon. Sarah was becoming less sure and could feel a lump in her chest. *I must stay positive*, she told herself firmly.

"Before you leave, I wanted to bring up something that several of you have talked to me about. Friday seems to be the worst day of the week for our meetings, what with summer coming and all. I wanted to ask if there was another day that would work better.

"How about Tuesday or Wednesday?" Allison called out. "I think the middle of the week would work better, at least for me."

"I don't work on Tuesday," Frank said, "so I wouldn't have to be late all the time."

"What do the rest of you think about changing to Tuesday?" Everyone appeared to agree, but Anna wasn't sure she was hearing from everyone, so she added, "Is that bad for anyone?" No one spoke. "Okay, then, we're the Tuesday Night Quilters effective next week.

"The TNQ," Anna said. "I like it. I'll get an email out to the members that weren't here tonight, and I'll see everyone on Tuesday.

On their way home, Sophie sighed and remarked, "That was fun. I should have listened to you years ago when you first started in on me about coming to these meetings."

"You weren't ready," Sarah responded as she turned and smiled at her very best friend. "You just weren't ready."

"Well, I am now," Sophie replied, sitting tall and looking extremely pleased with herself.

* * * * *

"John called while you were at your meeting last night," Charles said as they were having breakfast.

"Did he have any news?"

"Nothing encouraging," Charles responded. "If his contact is being honest with him, the FBI seems to be at a complete standstill. Ybarra swears he hasn't sent anyone after Laura Bradley, and they've offered several enticements to get him to talk."

"And still nothing?"

"Nothing."

"Actually," Sarah said thoughtfully, "I would think that if he were going to go after her, he would have done it long ago."

"True, but these guys get bored and look for ways to stir things up."

"And as you suggested, we may not be getting all the information the FBI has.

"True." Charles figured that the FBI was probably close to pulling out of the case and turning it over to Chicago PD. He knew that would happen once they officially determined it didn't involve a Federal case. He decided not to mention this to Sarah, although he and John had discussed the possibility.

Charles sighed and got up to refill his coffee cup. He lifted the lid on the cookie jar, but frowned and closed it.

"What are your plans for the day," Sarah asked as she stood to carry their dishes to the sink.

"As soon as they open, I'm going to the hardware store because I need to get a few keys made."

Sarah laughed. "And because you love hardware stores."

"That, too."

Chapter 23

When the phone rang, Sarah glanced at the display and saw that it was the Chicago Police Department.

"Hello?" she answered, wondering why they were calling and assuming it was for Charles.

"Sarah," the familiar voiced began, "This is Jake Krakowski from Chicago PD. How are you?"

"Detective Krakowski," she responded. "I'm fine. Charles isn't home right now, but ..."

"It's Jake, and I was hoping to speak with you."

"Oh?" she responded uncomfortably.

"I have something I want to ask you if you don't mind."

"Go ahead," she responded reluctantly.

"How well do you know Nathan Weaver?"

"Nathan?" she responded with surprise. "Ruth's husband? Well, I see him occasionally. Of course, I know him through Ruth but not personally. Why do you ask?"

"Have you been aware of any financial problems he might have."

"Ruth and I are quilting friends, but I don't know anything about their personal lives. I have no idea about their finances, except ... well, I do know he's been trying to get his computer business off the ground."

"What sort of computer business?" he asked.

"I have no idea. Have you talked with him?"

"I'm not ready to do that just yet. Do you know anyone who might know more about this business he's getting into?"

Sarah hesitated, wondering where the detective was going with this. "I know he's been working with his brother-in-law, Geoff Bailer. Geoff's married to Ruth's sister Anna. Geoff has a computer consulting business, and he's been helping Nathan get started. Why do you ask? Isn't this case in the hands of the FBI now?"

"It is, but I've had this nagging feeling that we're missing something. It started the day her husband came up here, and I can't get rid of it. There was something about his behavior, but I can't say what. Just an annoying feeling that he knew more than he was saying."

"I don't know what to tell you, Jake. He might be a little standoffish, but he seems like a nice guy, and he certainly was devastated by her kidnapping."

"I thought he seemed more terrified than devastated, Sarah."

"Well, that could be. I would be terrified *and* devastated if it were my loved one. You aren't suspecting him of being involved are you," she asked skeptically.

"I don't know. No. It's like I said before. I just feel something is off, and I wanted to run it passed you."

"Have you talked to the FBI about their investigation?"

"Yes, some."

"Why don't I have Charles call you when he gets home? He'd be a good person to run your concerns by, and he also knows Nathan and Geoff." She was hoping her husband would tell the detective the latest information he had about Dante Ybarra, but she had promised not to share that information with anyone.

As they were preparing to hang up, Sarah heard the garage door opening. "Wait a minute," she said to Jake. "I think I hear Charles now."

"It's Detective Krakowski," Sarah said as Charles came into the kitchen. "He'd like to talk with you."

Charles took the phone and said, "Hey, Jake. What's up?"

Sarah put the coffee pot on and listened to Charles' side of the conversation. He glanced at her once but didn't put the call on speaker.

"I hear what you're saying, Jake, but I think you've got to sit down with the guy."

There was another long pause while the detective talked, and then Charles said, "Sure, I could talk to him, but ultimately it's got to be you." They continued to talk for another few minutes, and Charles ended the conversation saying, "Okay, I'll see what I can do and get back to you."

He sighed when he hung up the phone and shook his head.

"What is it?" Sarah asked.

"He thinks there's some investigating to be done, and since your friend's case has been taken over by the FBI, his hands are tied. He said it isn't worth losing his retirement by going against his bosses, but he has a strong feeling that there's more to be learned."

"So he wants you to talk to Nathan?"

"That's it."

"Surely he doesn't think Nathan is involved in her disappearance. They are so much in love, Charles. . . ."

"I know, and that's not what he's saying. But he thinks Nathan knows something."

"Are you going to do it?"

"Got to, Sarah. He needs my help."

"You men in blue," she responded, shaking her head. "Always sticking together."

"It's the creed," he responded, pouring himself a cup of coffee and opening the cookie jar, only to find it still filled with his wife's latest find: low-fat, sugar-free wafers. He took two reluctantly.

* * * * *

Charles had been gone over an hour, and Sarah was getting jumpy. She wanted to know what it was Nathan knew and whether it would help someone find Ruth. She ran the vacuum and put a load of laundry in. Sometimes doing housework helped her deal with anxiety, but it wasn't working today.

In every room, she noticed things that could be used in a fidget quilt, and she began to collect them. She had a few wooden beads, a piece of lace, some fur she had kept when she had shortened the sleeves on a fake fur coat, some fringe, and a couple of crocheted doilies.

Sarah had already used the doll in the quilt she made at the meeting, but she remembered the party box she had in the garage with things left over from Alaina's second birthday party. In it, she found two little, soft bears. *I'll make a pocket with the fur piece*, she thought. An arrangement began to form in her mind. She looked in her fabric cabinet and found a piece of butterfly fabric and three others that coordinated with it nicely.

She checked the house phone and her cell phone to make sure there hadn't been any calls while she was in the garage. *Still no word from Charles.*

She grabbed a pad of paper and drew a rough design of the quilt she had in her head. She hurried to the sewing room and got to work cutting and stitching.

When she looked at what she had done, she frowned and said aloud, "It needs something." She wondered about a border but didn't want to make it any bigger since it would probably lay on someone's lap. "Prairie points," she suddenly exclaimed. She opened her laptop and did a computer search on making prairie points and was delighted when several tutorials popped up.

She stretched out her butterfly fabric and cut squares for the prairie points, which she decided to scatter around on the quilt rather than using them in the binding. She was preparing to add them to the quilt when she suddenly looked up and saw that it was early afternoon. She had worked right through lunch and was scheduled to teach a class at Stitches in forty-five minutes.

Leaving the room just as it was, she changed clothes, grabbed a peanut butter sandwich, and hurried to the garage. As she was pulling out of the community, she spotted Charles pulling in. There were no other cars around, so she drove close to the driver's side of his car and lowered her window and he did the same.

"You're leaving me?" he asked jocularly.

"No, you silly man. I've got a class to teach. I'll be back around dinner time. Pizza okay?"

"Always!" he responded, eager to take advantage of an opportunity to eat the good stuff. "Do you want me to order it?"

"I'll call it in after class and pick it up on my way home." His elation was short-lived. He could imagine the pizza that would make its way to his house that night.

"Broccoli and tofu with a touch of alfalfa sprout?" he responded playfully. Then in a more serious vein, he added, "I'll tell you about my meeting with Nathan when you get home."

"Is everything okay?" she asked.

"We'll have to wait and see. Good luck with your class." He blew her a kiss and they each drove off.

Chapter 24

"Jake, it's Charles Parker. I just left Nathan and he's on his way up to see you. You'll never believe what he had to say. You were right. He was holding something back—something big, in fact.

"And you're going to tell me, right?"

"No, Jake. This needs to come from him. He'll be there in a few hours. Don't go home."

"Thanks for getting this moving, Charles. I'll call you after I talk to him."

"You do that."

* * * * *

Charles wandered around the house for the next few hours, waiting for Sarah and eager to hear from Jake and Nathan. Walking down the hall, he noticed the light on Sarah's sewing machine and he went in to turn it off, realizing that she must have left in a hurry. He stopped to see what she was working on, but couldn't make sense of it. It didn't look like anything he'd seen her do before. *Lace? Bears?* His thoughts were interrupted by the phone.

"Charles, Nathan will be staying up here," Jake announced when Charles picked up the phone. "We're putting the wheels in motion."

"So you know these thugs he's talking about?" Charles asked.

"We sure do, and they *are* thugs but very organized and very dangerous. I can't go into it now but just sit tight. I'll let you know when something breaks."

* * * * *

"I'm in the living room," Charles called to Sarah when he heard her coming into the kitchen from the garage.

"I'll be right there," she responded. When she came into the living room, she was carrying the pizza box, a roll of paper towels, and two beers. "Dinner," she announced. They each reached for a piece of pizza and eagerly bit into it. Charles was pleased to see that the meat appeared to be real, and the vegetables were the familiar ones often found on a pizza. They had each devoured two pieces before Charles brought up the topic of his visit with Nathan.

Charles started talking about his call from Jake, but Sarah interrupted him as she reached for a napkin and slid the pizza box toward him indicating she was finished.

"Charles, you're confusing me. Start from the beginning. The last I heard, you were on your way to see Nathan. Start there."

"Okay, sorry. Nathan didn't want to talk to me at first, but he finally broke down, and the whole story started pouring out. He'd been having serious financial problems and was on the verge of losing his business. The bank had turned him down for any more loans, and he was afraid his troubles were going to spill over onto Ruth and her shop."

"Jake asked me about that, but I had no idea," Sarah responded. "Go on."

"Okay, so some guy that Nathan hardly knew told him about some easy money up in Chicago … 'Loans, no questions asked,' the guy had said."

"Surely Nathan knew better than to get involved in something like that."

"He was desperate, Sarah."

"Did Ruth know about this?"

"No, he didn't want to worry her. Anyway, he borrowed the money, and everything seemed fine for a while. He said he made his first few payments on time, and he didn't expect any trouble. Well, it turned out that he had gotten himself involved with a crime syndicate up there, and the interest started doubling every day until he owed the guys some astronomical amount that he'd never be able to pay." Charles smiled slightly when he added that Nathan said he figured they'd just threaten to break his knee caps.

"He watches too many movies," Sarah responded. "But what does all this have to do with Ruth's kidnapping?"

"They called him three weeks ago and said they had his wife and wouldn't release her until he paid them everything he owes, and at this point, it's several hundred thousand. He's been trying to come up with the money, but he's totally tapped out."

"Surely he went to the police."

"These goons told him they'd kill her if he went to the police. That's why he didn't tell Jake or the FBI."

"He hadn't told anyone?" she responded with alarm.

"Not until he talked to me today. I told him he had to tell Jake. I had to be frank with him about what could happen to his wife if he doesn't do something, and he finally agreed and left for Chicago a couple of hours ago."

"I wish you'd gone with him."

"I do too. I'm waiting now to hear from Jake."

"What does this mean for Tina Manchester or, I guess I should say, Laura Bradley?"

"It probably means that the FBI was on the wrong trail and moved the poor woman for nothing."

"What a way to live," Sarah responded sadly.

Charles finished off most of the pizza, and they waited for Jake's call.

"How about a cup of coffee?" Charles asked as they were clearing away the remnants of dinner.

"I'm jittery enough," she responded. "Let's sit down in the living room and watch a little television. It might help settle our nerves."

They both jumped when the phone rang, even though they'd been expecting the call.

Looking at the display as he picked up the phone, Charles told Sarah it was Nathan calling and he answered on speaker.

"Nathan, hello. Are you on your way home?"

"No, Charles, I'm here in the police station. Jake ran out and said he'd call me here when he knows something."

"You told him about the money and the threats, right?"

"Yes, and he knows the syndicate. Chicago PD Major Crimes has been trying to break into the organization for years. The good news is that they have an undercover agent inside, and Jake's hoping he can make contact with the guys that have Ruth."

"And he told you to wait there?"

"Yeah. Jake had a call from someone, told me to stay put, and took off about an hour ago. I'm frantic, Charles. What should I do?"

"You should do exactly what Jake told you to do. Sit tight. I wish I'd gone with you."

"Man, do I ever wish that too. This place gives me the willies, and what if there's gunfire and she gets killed. Charles, I can't stand this. It's my fault. I may have killed my wife."

"Okay, Nathan. First of all, don't say that in a police station. I know what you mean, but they won't. Second, you've got to trust that these guys know what they're doing. If Major Crimes is involved, you have the best of the best on the job. Just …"

"Wait a minute, Charles. Someone's here." Charles could hear voices in the background. Finally, Nathan returned to the phone. "There's an officer here who wants to take me to the hospital. He doesn't know why. He just said Detective Krakowski told him to pick me up and take me there." With a trembling voice, he added, "Oh, Charles, something has happened to my Ruth."

When Charles turned to Sarah, he saw that her face was white, and tears were streaming down her cheeks.

He wanted to take her in his arms and say, "Everything will be all right," but he knew he couldn't say that and mean it.

Chapter 25

The Cabin …

Ruth had tried to keep track of time. She knew she'd been in the cabin for at least three weeks.

She was beginning to feel panicked again. The men seemed to be getting restless. One day the man with the scar down his face had come down the cellar steps while Julio was there. He gave them both a nasty leer and said, "I'll bet you two are having a grand time down here." Ruth felt her skin crawl, and she began to tremble.

Then the man turned to Julio and said, "We're heading up the road for a while." Ruth hoped they wouldn't come back drunk. As he turned to leave, he looked over at Ruth again and sneered. "I wouldn't mind spending some time down here with this lovely lady." She heard them return in the middle of the night and prayed they wouldn't come down. They didn't.

A couple of days later as Julio was laying on the cot reading one of the books he had brought for Ruth, they heard a vehicle drive up. A few minutes later the cellar hatch was raised, and a man she hadn't seen before came down. He looked angry, and her panic returned.

"Hey, Lucas," Julio responded looking surprised to see the man. "What're you doing out here? We've already got more men on this than we need."

"You guys can all take off," the new man responded. "The boss sent me to take over. He wants you three at his place on the double. Sounds like something big's going down tonight."

Julio jumped up, ready for some excitement. The last three weeks had been boring, to say the least. But then he looked at Ruth and saw her mounting fear. Her eyes seemed to be pleading with him not to leave her alone with this man. Somehow he had become her protector, and he didn't like the role. It was making him soft.

"Look out for this lady," Julio said, unable to just throw her to the wolves. "The boss doesn't want anything to happen to her."

"You got it," the man responded coldly.

"You'll be okay," Julio said, looking back at Ruth as he was leaving the cellar. "Lucas is an okay guy."

She listened as the van pulled away and with trepidation glanced over at the man called Lucas and saw that he now had a reassuring smile on his face. He didn't look frightening any longer. "You're going to be just fine, Ruth," he said. "It's almost over."

Ruth, feeling that something had changed, looked directly into his eyes and spoke for the first time. "Who are you?" she asked.

"My undercover name is Lucas Whitmore, Chicago PD," he responded, and she gasped. She felt confusion, fear, and hope simultaneously. "Just hang on a little longer," he added. "They're on their way."

At that moment, the front door crashed open above them, and heavy boots stomped across the floor. "You down there, Lucas?" a voice called.

"We're here, and the woman is fine."

They could hear the cellar door being lifted and the team, running in lockstep, poured into the cellar. "You folks okay?" one of the men asked and, without waiting for an answer, added "Come on. Let's get this woman out of here."

"What about the others?" Lucas asked.

"We picked them up on the road a few hundred yards from here. They're all three in custody and obviously ready to talk. As a matter of fact," he added with a chuckle, "they were eager to tell us that this was all your idea."

"Won't they be surprised?" Lucas responded, helping Ruth up and wrapping a blanket around her shoulders. "Let's get this young lady some medical attention."

"I'm fine. I just want to go home."

"Your husband is meeting us at the hospital," the officer responded.

"It's over," Lucas reassured her as he gently led her toward the stairs.

Ruth turned to him and said, "That one man, Julio, he was kind to me."

"You'll have a chance to get that into the record, but these are all bad dudes. We've been after them for years. They'll get what they deserve."

* * * * *

The doctor told Nathan to wait until the medical staff had completed their examination of his wife. The officer that drove him to the hospital was sitting with him, trying to keep him calm and explaining that Detective Krakowski would be speaking with Ruth next, and then Nathan could see her.

Just a few rooms up the hall, Jake Krakowski was looking at the small woman lying in the bed. She seemed anxious, yet exhausted. The doctor had assured the detective that there were no signs of brutality, and he was relieved.

He introduced himself and told her that her husband was waiting to see her.

"May I see him now?" she pleaded.

"I need to ask you a few questions first, but believe me, Mrs. Weaver, you're safe now. The men have been arrested, and you'll be going home just as soon as the doctor releases you.

"Today?" she asked hopefully.

"I'm sure you'll go home today. Do you feel like telling me what happened?"

"There was so much …"

"Just start from the beginning," he said patiently as he pulled up a chair and sat close to the bed.

She told him about going to her van and being grabbed by the man. She stopped to ask the detective if her friend Sarah was okay and he assured her that Sarah and Tessa were both fine. Ruth went on to describe the cellar where they held her and what happened there. "I'm not sure I remember everything," she said apologetically. She told them about the kind man, Julio. "I think he was protecting me from the others," she added.

She told him about Lucas' arrival and the SWAT team and then she closed her eyes for a few minutes. When she opened them, she said, "That's all I can remember."

He thanked her and handed her his card. He asked that she call him if she thought of anything else and she said she would.

"Will I have to testify?" she asked.

"It's very likely, but don't think about that now."

"Who were these men?" she asked. "Why did they take me?"

"I'm not the one to tell you why you were taken, but I can tell you what took us so long to find you. He explained about the FBI and the U.S. Marshal's investigation.

"Why were *they* looking for me? I'm not that important. ..."

He gave her a weak smile, knowing that the experience had robbed her of her confidence. Crimes like this often left the victim confused about their own self-worth. But everything he had learned about her convinced him she'd fight her way back.

"The FBI took over the case because they thought you were taken by mistake. It seems that you look very much like a woman who was in the witness protection program." He went on to tell her the whole story, and she listened intently.

"So that poor lady, they gave her a new identity and moved her away because of me?"

"Not because of you, Ruth. They moved her to protect her. They thought this Dante Ybarra would try again once they realized they had the wrong person. But they were wrong about the whole thing. It wasn't Ybarra behind your kidnapping."

"But who *was* it? If it wasn't this Ybarra, then who was it and why? Why me?"

They both looked up when the door opened at that moment. Nathan Weaver looked at his wife, his face twisted with agony. "I did this to you," he muttered as he took her in his arms. He began to sob, "I'm so sorry ... so sorry."

Jake left the room. *That man is riddled with guilt,* he told himself. He wondered if she would forgive him. He suspected she would.

Chapter 26

"I don't know why we couldn't see her until today," Sophie complained as Sarah parked the car in the handicapped space outside the quilt shop. It was Tuesday night, and everyone had been told to come prepared to celebrate Ruth's return.

"She needed time to be with her husband and find her way. This has been a devastating experience for her. Jake said she could benefit from victim counseling, but she told me she wants to wait and see how she's feeling."

"You've seen her?" Sarah asked.

"No, but we spent an hour on the phone Sunday night. She didn't say much about what she's been through. I don't think she's ready to talk about it. She's just glad to be home."

"Did she mention Nathan?"

"Only to say he made dinner that night."

"Well, that means he's still living there," Sophie concluded.

"They've been through a lot together over the years, Sophie. I think it would take more than this to break them apart. They love each other. In fact, they loved each other enough to walk away from their community and the Amish way of life. I think they're committed. Besides, he borrowed the money because he was afraid his business debts might cause her to lose the shop. He didn't know all this could happen as a result."

"I hope no one asks about all this tonight," Sophie said.

"It's a party," Sarah responded. "I don't think they will."

When they walked in, they could immediately see it was going to be a festive occasion. All the quilt club members were there, even ones they hadn't seen for months. Sarah glanced around but didn't see Ruth. As she was pouring punch for herself and Sophie, who was now sitting on one of the chairs that had been placed in somewhat of a circle in the main part of the shop, she heard the front door bell jingling and turned to look.

Ruth was standing there dressed in a soft blue pantsuit with a pastel multicolored silk scarf fashionably draped around her neckline. Nathan was standing close by her with his arm around her shoulders. Sarah noticed that Ruth's arm was lovingly wrapped around his waist. She glanced at Sophie, who gave her an almost imperceptible wink. *They will be fine*, she thought as she smiled at Sophie.

"So what have you folks been working on while I was away?" Ruth asked, dismissing the few sympathetic overtures that were made and walking into the center of a group of friends.

"Fidget quilts," Frank called out. "We made fidget quilts."

"What?" Ruth exclaimed. "Really?" she asked, looking at Sarah.

"Really," Sarah responded.

"Thank you," Ruth mouthed soundlessly, and she headed for the work table where all the fidget quilts were displayed.

"I can't believe you did this. Aren't they wonderful? Look, Nate," she added as she explained the concept to him.

Sophie told her about the two she took to the nursing home and that the staff was ecstatic. "They want more as soon as we can make them," she added.

"I thought about these while I was away," Ruth said in a tone of voice one might use when they just returned from a business trip. "I tried to figure out how to attach them and how to finish the quilt, and I see you folks solved all that. These are wonderful. Oh, and you made dresses for the dolls and even for the cat," she exclaimed.

"We did that," Penny announced. She had come to the meeting with Caitlyn, who promised to teach her how to quilt. Caitlyn had asked Sarah if Penny could come, and Sarah said she could come any time she wanted. Ruth looked at the young girl as if she were trying to remember who she was.

"You two haven't met officially," Sophie said, "but she's been in the shop with me. "Ruth, this is my granddaughter, Penelope.... Oh, I'm so sorry, honey." Penny was clearly fuming about being called Penelope. "I mean this is my granddaughter, Penny Ward."

"I'm very happy to meet you, Miss Ward. Are you a quilter?"

"Not yet," she responded, "but I'm going to learn."

"Well, you come in here and take some classes," Ruth said. "We offer beginning quilting classes every few months."

They didn't get around to their regular meeting for another hour or so. They had spent most of the time laughing and enjoying the fact that they were all back together again.

Sarah had called Charles and asked him to come by, thinking that Nathan was feeling a bit out of place. Once he arrived, Charles became the center of attention for a while, as he always did when he was in a group of women. He finally turned to Nathan and said, "Let's grab a beer at Barney's and let these quilters get to work. Do you want to join us, Frank?"

Frank dropped his eyes and blushed. "I don't drink beer. Could I get a Coke?"

"Sure thing. We'll see you folks later," he called as the three went out the door. Sarah noticed Frank was walking especially tall, obviously proud to be one of the guys.

Everyone was too excited to work, but they pulled out the box of accoutrements and began choosing the ones they wanted to use on their next fidget quilts. "Let's look around at home and see what we can find to add to our collection," Sarah suggested.

"And I'd like to go to a craft supply store and poke around," Ruth said. "I need some shopping time, and also I've had some ideas for how we could make these for men as well. I want to get some John Deere fabric, maybe some miniature tools, and I'd like to figure out how to fashion something that looks like a tool belt."

"I love that idea," Myrtle called from the back of the room. "My husband's been down with this old-timers thing for a while now. He doesn't recognize anyone but me anymore, and he can be a real handful. I'd love to make something like that for him." Sarah could hear enthusiasm in her voice but saw traces of sadness in her eyes.

As the meeting was breaking up, Sophie called to Sarah saying, "Andy's here to pick up Caitlyn and Penny. I think I'll ride home with them."

"Fine," Sarah responded. "I'll see you tomorrow for coffee and stitching."

As soon as everyone had left the shop except Sarah and Charles, Ruth asked them to stay for a few minutes. "I want to thank you, Charles. Nathan told me what you did, and I realize that without you, I might still be in that cellar."

"Not true, Ruth. Nathan knew what to do, and he would have done it without my encouragement. He was just afraid for your safety. Those thugs told him not to go to the police."

"That's true," Nathan said as he came out of the storage room where he'd been restacking the folding chairs. "I knew the FBI was involved. If they hadn't been so secretive about what they were doing, I could have told them they were on the wrong track. I tried to talk to them, and they dismissed me, saying they were on the trail of the men who took you and I should go home and wait. I figured they knew what they were doing and would have you home in no time. I had no idea they were on the wrong trail."

"Well, it's over now," Ruth said with a certain finality in her voice.

"And it's time to celebrate," Sarah replied as she reached into her tote bag and pulled out a bottle of champagne and four glasses.

Epilogue

Five years later …

Laura Bradley, a.k.a. Tina Manchester, a.k.a. Teresa Lang, and now Laura Bradley again—the name she was born with—sat in her bungalow on the outskirts of her hometown and looked out over the valley and the mountains beyond, a view she had looked at from this very room for the first twenty-two years of her life. She smiled as she thought about the call from the U.S. Marshal: "Dante Ybarra is dead. It's over. You can go home."

She didn't ask how he died. She didn't care. It was over.

Laura hummed softly as she walked throughout the house, opening the windows and letting freedom float in on the light summer breeze.

See full quilt on back cover.

THE FIDGET QUILT

The Friday Night Quilters made "fidget quilts" for the local nursing home. Embellish this 24˝ × 24˝ quilt with your choice of trim: from rickrack to zippers to a pocket with a stuffed animal.

MATERIALS

Fabric squares:

9 squares 8½˝ × 8½˝ in assorted prints

19 squares 4˝ × 4˝ for prairie points*

Assorted trims and notions: For embellishments

Backing: ⅞ yard

Batting: 28˝ × 28˝

Binding: ¼ yard

* Back cover quilt has 19 prairie points, but you may make as many or few as desired. (See Tip, page 210, for positioning the prairie points.)

Tip || Securely attach all embellishments. Nothing should pose a choking hazard or risk being dropped and lost.

PROJECT

Project Instructions

Seam allowances are ¼".

MAKE PRAIRIE POINTS

1. Fold a prairie-point square in half diagonally, wrong sides together. Press.

2. Fold in half again across the long, folded edge. Press.

3. Repeat Steps 1 and 2 for your desired number of prairie points.

> **Tip** ‖ Before the quilt assembly, decide where you want prairie points. Sandwich them, aligning the raw edges, between the right sides of blocks or rows before stitching. Stitch and press as usual. Note that each prairie point overlaps the one before it by half at its base.

ASSEMBLE AND FINISH THE QUILT

1. Sew 3 fabric squares together into a row. Make 3 rows.

2. Sew the rows together.

3. Layer the pieced top with batting and backing. Quilt as desired.

4. Place the prairie points between the binding and the quilt top, if desired. Bind the quilt.

5. Embellish the quilt as desired.

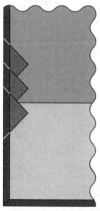

Position prairie points between
binding and quilt top before stitching.

Turn the page for a preview ----------------------------➔
of the next book in A Quilting Cozy series.

PROJECT

2nd edition includes instructions to make the featured quilt

Tattered & Torn

a quilting cozy

Carol Dean Jones

Preview of
Tattered & Torn

"Do you know anything about this old quilt?" Sarah asked as she gently ran her fingers over the delicate pattern, hesitant to even pick it up for fear it might crumble. "It looks very old."

"My guess would be that it's fifty or sixty years old," the shopkeeper responded, "but I don't know anything about it. It just came in a couple of weeks ago, and I haven't had a chance to examine it closely."

Sarah didn't make a habit of trolling thrift shops like her many friends in the retirement community where she lived, but this quilt had caught her eye as she was strolling past the shop on her way to meet her friend Sophie at the nearby café.

The shopkeeper carefully picked the quilt up and spread it out across an equally old upholstered wing chair. "The fabrics appear to be old, but I'm really not very knowledge-able about quilts. If you're interested in it, you might want to talk to someone in the quilt shop up the street." She slipped her glasses on and looked at it more closely. "Look at these tiny stitches," she said. "I haven't had it appraised," she added thoughtfully, "but I probably should before selling it."

Sarah examined the quilt carefully, noting places where the fabrics had partially disintegrated and other places where patterns were faded beyond recognition. She thought about the woman who had tediously pieced the quilt using scraps from her family's worn-out clothing. *It's amazing it has lasted this long*, she thought as she carefully lifted an edge to examine the back.

"I'd like to buy it," she found herself saying. The two women discussed it and ultimately agreed on a price, despite the shopkeeper's hesitance to sell it. Sarah had already begun wondering whether she could make the necessary repairs.

As she was leaving the shop with her carefully wrapped bundle securely tucked under her arm, Sarah turned to the shopkeeper and asked, "How did you happen to come by this quilt?"

"A woman brought it to me just a few weeks ago. She said her husband found it in the attic of an old building they were demolishing—part of the downtown revitalization program. They're tearing down public housing and replacing it with high-priced condominiums."

"I've read about that, and I've wondered where the people who were living there were going …" Sarah replied thoughtfully.

"To shelters and the streets would be my guess," the woman responded.

"The whole thing doesn't leave me feeling particularly *revitalized*," Sarah replied with a sigh as she left the shop and headed for the café.

On the way, Sarah passed the quilt shop and decided to stop in for a minute and show the quilt to her friend Ruth, the owner of Running Stitches.

"I only have a minute," Sarah began as she opened the bag and laid the quilt on the counter still folded. "I'm meeting Sophie, but I wanted you to see this. The owner of the shop said it was probably fifty or sixty years old."

"Sarah, you have a real treasure here, and I'm surprised Florence didn't realize what she had. From these fabrics, I'd say this quilt dates back to the mid-1800s, probably before the Civil War."

"Really?" Sarah gasped. "She said it's a hexagon quilt. Did they make them that long ago?"

"Hexagon quilt patterns became popular back in the 1700s, and there are many different layouts and names—the most common being this pattern, Grandmother's Flower Garden. And these fabrics were very common during the Civil War period. This is an exciting find, Sarah."

"Would you help me figure out how to repair it?"

Ruth hesitated. "I'd be happy to talk with you about it, but you might not want to disturb its authenticity."

Sarah was eager to continue the conversation, but at that moment several customers were entering the shop. Sarah knew Sophie was probably becoming impatient, so she slipped the quilt back into the bag and told Ruth she'd be back.

"Come by early in the morning," Ruth said as her friend was leaving, and Sarah nodded her agreement.

* * * * *

"That thing is in shreds!" her boisterous buddy bellowed when Sarah revealed the contents of her package. "Why would you pay good money for that rag? I could have given you something I use in Emma's dog bed if I had known you wanted something like this."

"Sophie, this *rag* as you call it is a piece of our history. It may well be a priceless antique."

"*Priceless* is right. There's no price a sane person would pay for it."

Sophie was new to the world of quilting, and Sarah knew to be patient with her, but she was finding it challenging. She repackaged her treasure and over lunch began sharing some of the stories she had heard about quilts created during the Civil War period.

Sarah told her friend about how fancy quilts were made and sold to raise money for the war effort and how simpler quilts were made as cot quilts for sons and husbands as they headed out to join the fighting. When she got to the part about how often the bodies of their loved ones were wrapped and buried in these simple quilts, Sophie became quiet. "Sorry," she muttered contritely. "I didn't know."

"Very few quilts made in that period have survived; if this is truly one of them, it's a real treasure. I just wish I knew more about its history."

Sophie was quiet as they drove home, and Sarah knew to give her friend the space she needed. As Sophie was getting out of the car, she turned to Sarah and said, "If you want to find out where this quilt came from, I'd like to help you."

"Great," Sarah responded enthusiastically. "The Sarah-Sophie investigation team is on the job."

Sophie threw her head back and cackled, instantly returning to her usual outrageous self. "We're going to be detecting again. Shall I bring my gun?"

"Sophie, you know you don't have a gun, and we wouldn't need it for this job even if you did."

READER'S GUIDE:
A QUILTING COZY SERIES
by Carol Dean Jones

1. The quilts which were ultimately displayed in the Silent Voices exhibit offered Alzheimer's victims and caregivers the opportunity to express feelings for which they had no words. As you read the descriptions of the various quilts, did you get a sense for what feelings the quilters might have been trying to express? Do you think this experience helped the people suffering from Alzheimer's? The caregivers?

2. The man who saw Ruth struggling with her attacker was on his way to the airport and chose not to report it to the police. Charles said there is a fine line between interfering in other people's lives and doing the responsible thing. What would you have done in this situation?

3. How do you think a fidget quilt could bring comfort to a person suffering dementia? Would this be a useful charity project for quilt groups or crafters? What items would you include?

4. Why do you think the author chose to place Julio (the 'kind man') among Ruth's captors?

5. Timothy and Andy both found themselves as single fathers of teenage girls late in life. Discuss how they were able to excel at their new responsibilities.

6. Do you think Ruth will be able to forgive Nathan for the part he played in her kidnapping? How could he have prevented it?

A Note
from the Author

I hope you enjoyed *Missing Memories* as much as I enjoyed writing it. This is the eighth book in A Quilting Cozy Series and is followed by *Tattered & Torn*, which includes a vintage quilt found in a thrift shop, an exhaustive search through the past, and a murder suspect, all interwoven as the Cunningham Village friends return in this ninth book of the series, promising mystery, friendship, and lots of quilting.

On page 212, I have included a preview to *Tattered & Torn* so that you can get an idea of what our cast of characters will be involved in next.

Please let me know how you are enjoying this series. I love hearing from my readers and encourage you to contact me on my blog or send me an email.

Best wishes,

Carol Dean Jones
caroldeanjones.com
quiltingcozy@gmail.com

A Quilting Cozy Series by Carol Dean Jones

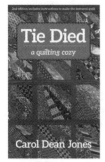

2nd edition includes instructions to make the featured quilt

Tie Died
a quilting cozy

Carol Dean Jones

2nd edition includes instructions to make the featured quilt

Running Stitches
a quilting cozy

Carol Dean Jones

2nd edition includes instructions to make the featured quilt

Sea Bound
a quilting cozy

Carol Dean Jones

2nd edition includes instructions to make the featured quilt

Patchwork Connections
a quilting cozy

Carol Dean Jones

2nd edition includes instructions to make the featured quilt

Stitched Together
a quilting cozy

Carol Dean Jones

2nd edition includes instructions to make the featured quilt

Moon Over the Mountain
a quilting cozy

Carol Dean Jones

2nd edition includes instructions to make the featured quilt

The Rescue Quilt
a quilting cozy

Carol Dean Jones

2nd edition includes instructions to make the featured quilt

Missing Memories
a quilting cozy

Carol Dean Jones

2nd edition includes instructions to make the featured quilt

Tattered & Torn
a quilting cozy

Carol Dean Jones

2nd edition includes instructions to make the featured quilt

Left Holding the Bag
a quilting cozy

Carol Dean Jones

Includes instructions to make the featured quilt

Beneath Missouri Stars
a quilting cozy

Carol Dean Jones

Includes instructions to make the featured quilt

Frayed Edges
a quilting cozy

Carol Dean Jones